Matter
OF
TIME

The Hart Series

book six

M.E. CARTER

Matter of Time

The Hart Series

book six

ONE
Nicole

"You were flirting with him! I saw you!" He grabs my arm and begins squeezing, the strength of his fingertips digging into my skin. My heart races as I plead.

"He asked me where the bathroom was. I was just answering his question!"

His face contorts, his eyes darkening. He looks like pure evil. "So you could go with him and blow him? Huh? Answer me! Do you want his dick in your mouth?"

"No!" I yell, but he's not listening, too enraged to calm down. "It's you I love! You!"

"You're mine, do you understand? MINE!"

My cheekbone feels like it explodes as he backhands my face. I have no doubt my skin has broken open. The blood is already oozing down my cheek.

"How dare you make me hit you like this. This is all your fault!"

He roars with anger and... I startle awake, my face pressing so hard into the pillow that my cheek aches.

I quickly run my hand down my face. No blood.

"It wasn't real," I whisper to myself. "Only a nightmare."

Finally satisfied I'm safe in my apartment, I roll onto my back and *breathe in... two, three, four... hold, two, three, four... and out, two, three, four... hold.* My heart begins to calm and the normal sounds around me start to register.

Another roar from outside my door and I finally put together what loud noises woke me up.

Trivia Night at Frui Vita.

Grabbing the remote, I turn my small television off and slide my jeans on. I'm not sure how I fell asleep on the couch. I usually don't go to bed until the bar is closed. I must be extra tired tonight. The last thing I remember is someone named Alex being added to *The Circle*. I didn't stay awake long enough to find out if he's a catfish.

This is what my life has come to. Living in a small apartment in the back of my almost brother-in-law's bar and binge-watching reality television every night. Pathetic. At some point, I need to look at moving on with my life. It's been months since I left my jerk boyfriend, Jeremy. While he still plagues me in nightmares, I want to have a life when I'm awake, not be stuck in this limbo I've found myself in.

Making sure I have my keys, I head out the door locking it behind me. My makeup probably looks awful and my hair is piled on top of my head, but whatever. It's late and I doubt I know any of the customers tonight. Heath and his football team are still away at training camp and with the exception of a few others, they are the only guys I know. And only because Heath is my nephew's godfather so he's always around.

I ease my way up to the bar and sit on the stool that I claimed months ago. I've got my back to a wall, my side to the counter, and I can see every inch of the large room. I feel safest sitting here. I'm also out of the way while my sister works.

Somehow though, she always knows when I join her. I don't even say hello before she's setting a glass of Sprite down in front of me.

"Thanks." I lean on the bar and take a sip of my non-alcoholic beverage, observing the team play happening near the stage. The guys at one of the tables are wearing matching neon green shirts. It makes me smile. "How's Trivia Night going?"

Kiersten wipes her hands on a towel and grabs the shaker. I'm always in awe watching her work. She's only been here a little over a year and has multi-tasking down pat. "Busy as always."

Frui Vita is a low-key establishment that caters to the professional athletes in the area, and there are a lot of them. The outside of this place looks like a random dive bar on the side of the road. But the inside is gorgeous with its wood beams and black accents. It's become a favorite stop for the people who want to let their hair down without being bombarded with fans or people taking shady pictures to sell to the tabloids later.

"Which team is that?" I ask, tipping my head toward the guys in green. I barely get the question out before more cheers erupt and a huge guy with floppy blond hair stands up so quickly his chair falls backward. He raises his hands in victory, teammates holding their drinks up to give him their salute.

My sister just shakes her head with a smirk. "That would be the Slingers hockey team. Kade said they start preseason in a couple of weeks so apparently tonight is one last hurrah before hitting the ice hard for the next few months."

"Kade? Is he here tonight?" I pray my cheeks aren't turning pink just from saying his name. Too many people are in my business now as it is. I don't want to tip them off that I may have developed a small crush on their newest bartender.

It's not even a realistic crush. More like a fantasy of who he might be. If I've learned anything in the last couple of years, it's that fantasy and reality are never the same. Ever. So, while I can indulge in a little unrequited interest from afar, I'm not dumb enough to pretend the Kade in my head is the true Kade. I'll never make that mistake with any man again.

Kiersten finishes her mixing and pours the liquid into a martini glass. "He's in the back taking a minute before we get another wave of orders. It's been non-stop."

Biting my lip, I contemplate pitching an idea to my sister. I've been thinking about it for a while. Maybe I need to go for it. Like my therapist, Dr. Rhonda would say, what's the worst that can happen?

Actually, I know the answer to that. I've lived it. I have to push past those fears though, because in this context they're not realistic. Instead, I take a deep breath and toss out my idea before I lose my courage.

"I was thinking, if the offer is still good, maybe I could help you guys out some. I need to do more than just hang out with you and watch television, you know? Maybe start earning some money for my own place." Kiersten whips her head around to look at me, jaw practically falling to the floor. "But only if you need someone. Not, like as a charity case or whatever..." I tack on quietly regretting that I opened up this conversation. I have no idea how Kiersten is going to react. She's always made it clear I was welcome to work here. Paul, the owner of this place and her live-in boyfriend, has too. Up until now, I've always turned them down, so I'm not surprised by her initial reaction. What I don't know is if she's going to play this cool, or if she's going to do her big sister version of therapy. I'm hoping it's the former.

To her credit, she pulls herself together and continues on with what she was doing. "We could always use help these days. I know Paul is talking about finally getting the kitchen renovated so we can add more menu options besides pretzels and peanuts. That doesn't actually help you now, I just forgot to tell you earlier."

"Oh." I twist my lips, disappointed they don't have something more immediate. "Well, I guess just let me know when he needs someone in the kitchen. I'm sure I can figure out how to deep fry chicken strips or whatever."

"Nicole, I didn't say we don't need help now. You just reminded me that more is coming as well. We may have almost doubled the staff around here in the last few months but that still means there are only five of us."

"We may be back down to four soon," a male voice says as he slides behind the bar.

Kade.

Please cheeks, don't blush. You don't know him. He could be a massive jerk like Jeremy. Don't get in too deep.

"Oh, hey Nicole." Kade flashes me a kind smile then immediately gets back to work, grabbing a stack of bowls and filling them with peanuts.

Kiersten on the other hand has her hands on her hips. "What does that mean? Are you quitting?"

"No, but I overheard Sandra arguing with her husband

about how late she works."

Kiersten rolls her eyes so far back in her head it's a wonder they don't get stuck there. "This is a *bar*, not Chuck-E-Cheese. What were they expecting?"

Kade shrugs. "The way it sounded, she knew what she was getting into but he's not having it."

A shiver runs down my spine and I say a silent prayer that Sandra isn't in the same kind of situation I was. I know better than to ask her directly. She probably wouldn't admit it if there was a deeper problem anyway. The only thing I can do is hope she reads the signs posted in the restroom about getting out of a bad situation and jots down the number in case she needs it.

Turning to me, Kiersten continues to purse her lips in irritation. "Looks like we have a waitressing job opening up soon. Interested?"

I want to say yes. I want to jump at the chance to take back my independence and make some money to start planning my future. I want to more than I've wanted almost anything in a very long time.

But I can't. I'm frozen, thinking about what happens when I walk out in the middle of that room, amongst all those people, all those very large men who are drinking and partying. My breathing starts to pick up as the anxiety of a moment that hasn't even happened takes over.

I shake my head, partly to force my body to move and partly to answer my sister. "I think it would be better to wait for that kitchen job."

Kiersten's face falls. She knows she hit a trigger; she just doesn't know how. "What? No, I don't want you to do that." She puts her hand on my arm, her signature move when she's trying to show her support of me. "Is it because of all the guys? We can make sure you only work when

Paul does so you have back up, or I don't know, we can figure something out."

"I can be the waiter."

Kiersten and I both look up at Kade who is drying a glass now that's he done with the peanuts.

"You would… why would you do that?" I tilt my head to the side, curious about his answer.

I can tell he's going for nonchalance but something about the way he moves his hands, maybe because he keeps wiping the glass over and over, has me feeling like he's nervous. But why?

He licks his lips and swallows slowly. "I can deliver drinks and take orders. If it means you get to stay behind the bar and have some distance between yourself and all that mess." He looks out into the room, the noise down to a low hum as everyone concentrates on whatever answer they're searching for.

I, on the other hand, can't take my eyes off Kade. He's not tall and he's a little thicker around the middle than maybe he should be. His glasses have a tendency to slide down his nose and his hair always sticks up in weird ways. He is not what most people would describe as super-hot, but I imagine hugging him would be like being held by a teddy bear—warm and comfortable and most of all, safe. Like nothing outside his embrace can touch me.

I know that's probably not realistic, but regardless, in my eyes, he's a true gentleman in a world full of jerks. And my crush has ratcheted up a notch.

Careful there, I think to myself. *One nice thing doesn't mean he's a saint.*

I offer him a quick smile. "Thank you, Kade."

"Yes, thank you." Kiersten's voice sounds boisterous after my almost whisper-like answer. "I'll talk to Paul about the wage part of the job and see what he has to say."

"It's no problem." Kade glances back over at me one more time, his cheeks tinting the slightest shade of pink, and gets back to work.

Kiersten takes the opportunity to turn back to me, excitement dancing in her eyes. "So you'll do it? You'll take the bartender position?"

I only hesitate for a few seconds, long enough to pretend I'm taking a sip of my Sprite when really I'm allowing my anxious thoughts to settle back into their tiny space in my brain before answering.

"Yes. I'll take the job."

Kiersten squeals just like I knew she would. I wish I had even a small portion of the enthusiasm she has about me venturing back out into the world. Because as determined as I am to do this, it's going to be one of the hardest things I've ever done.

TWO

Kade

“**C**ome on, little guy,” I say quietly as I scoop up the cricket who accidentally got inside. His chirping has been driving me crazy, but even more so, I know he'll get squished if I don't toss him outside.

“Quit hopping around, man. I'm trying to save your life.” I finally get him in my hand and enclose my fingers around him. Crickets are one of the only types of insect that don't freak me out, even with him trying to hop around inside my fist.

Quickly, I throw him outside into the small grassy area next to the door. My mission finally accomplished, I head back to my station, behind the bar at Frui Vita, my place of employment.

I've been working here for about six months and enjoy it for the most part. The pay is great, my boss is fantastic, and no one can say I don't get enough social interaction. That's practically all I do here—socialize with customers.

For the most part, everyone else who works here is

great, too. Thank God it's Tammy waitressing tonight, though. Sandra was fine, but I knew she was short-lived. I find it hard to enjoy working with someone when you can see the writing on the wall and know they'll be leaving you in a lurch again soon.

I never knew I had this judgmental quirk until Paul gave me this job. Now that I've been here for so long and we've gone through several waitresses, I'm finding it harder to want to get to know the new employees. Why put in the effort when we're going to get screwed in the end anyway?

I glance over to the end of the bar and see the only person I have the opposite problem with.

Nicole.

She has a curious look on her face and when I accidentally make eye contact, her cheeks pinken and she quickly looks away. I'm not sure what that's about, but I suspect it's because she's a bit on the shy side. Not painfully so, but enough that even with how often she's here, we haven't gotten to know each other that well.

I'm hoping that will change soon. She's getting ready to start working here and is hanging around almost every night to just observe. It's not like it's a hard commute since she lives in the back apartment. But I have this feeling she's excited about getting started, too. I just hope I can maintain some sort of distance when she does.

Not that I'm an aggressive guy, quite the opposite. I just like being near her. From what I've learned over the course of the months, she's got a friendly smile for everyone, she's witty when she finally feels comfortable talking to someone, and she is easily entertained just by people watching. More than once I've noticed her cheer when Dwayne, our human mascot beats someone at pool, or laugh when some rookie is getting hazed by their teammates.

More and more I've found myself wanting to get to know everything about her—her likes, her dislikes, her dreams, her fears. Hell, I even want to know what size shoe she wears. That's how into her I am.

Not that I will ever ask for any of that information. Nicole looks like a bombshell and is the sweetest person I've ever met. She deserves so much more than a loser geek like me. She needs to be wined and dined and be covered in jewelry. I prefer video games and Chex Mix and indulge in a Ring Pop every now and then. I'm not at all her type.

No, what she needs is a man like the ones who frequent this bar. They all have money and success. And they're all very athletic. That's the kind of man she deserves. Someone who can take care of her and provide for her every desire. I want that for her. I'm hoping when she starts in a couple of days it'll be the beginning of her finding that perfect person. It's going to hurt like a bitch to watch, but I'm willing as long as she's happy.

I finish wiping down the counter as my pseudo-brother Jaxon approaches and leans against the wood top.

"What's up?"

"I just need a Shiner. And do you have any limes?" He leans over the counter like he can see behind it even though he can't.

"Sure. Coming up."

It's rare to see Jaxon here anymore. Now that he's started his clinics for medical school he's either at the hospital, in the library, or sleeping. His wife Annika shows up more than he does and she hates the bar scene, for reasons I'm unsure of. Not that it's my business anyway.

After grabbing his drink from the small fridge and popping the top, I add a lime wedge to the rim and hand Jaxon his beer. He immediately shoves the wedge inside and takes a long drink before letting out a sigh of contentment.

"How's it going?" he asks. I'm not all that surprised he's making small talk. His best friend, Heath Germaine, is at training camp with the San Antonio Steer so the usual crowd Jaxon runs with isn't here, and since Annika is a sports trainer for the same team, she went with them. Jaxon must really be lonely if he's here by himself.

"At work or school?"

His body sags onto a stool, no tension to be seen now that's he's got his bottle. "Both."

"School is fine. The semester just started and it's more basic requirements so it's not hard. And work is fine. Everyone is still nice. The customers still seem happy. And Paul is still a great boss."

Jaxon tilts his head in a partial nod. "That he is. I know he likes you working here."

The comment is unexpected. "He does? How do you know that?"

"He really struggles trying to find a good fit. Doesn't want to mess with the vibe of the place so he'd have to like you to keep you around."

I understand exactly what Jaxon means. The vast majority of Frui Vita's customers are professional athletes and their friends. One of the things they seem to like about me is that I don't really have any interest in sports. I'm trying to learn more now that I work here, but it isn't something I have any desire to get deeply involved with. Makes it hard to find common ground when I work, but apparently it also gives the customers a stronger sense of anonymity or something.

"Hey, as long as they're happy with my work ethic and

think I fit in well enough, it's fine by me."

"That's exactly why Paul likes you." Jaxon begins absentmindedly peeling the label off his beer and I know he has something more on his mind. "So, when are you going to do something about that?"

"About what?"

He points his beer bottle at Nicole. "About your feelings for Nicole."

"I don't… There's not…What feelings?" I finally manage to sputter.

I'm sure my face turns bright red. I can feel the heat rising from my neck. I hope it just looks like I'm flushed from work. Doubt it, though.

Jaxon chuckles, not deceived at all. "You can't hide the fact that you're half in love with her from me. I'm your brother."

He's actually not my brother. For a while, we thought we shared a biological father since his birth dad cheated on his wife with my mom. DNA proved we were wrong.

While I still don't know who my father is, Jaxon decided genetics don't matter anyway and that was that. I'm not sure if he ever told his mom and adoptive dad the truth, but they brought me into their family fold anyway. Mostly just for holidays.

It's not like I have any other family that gives a shit about me. Mom has always been too busy living her life to actually care what I'm up to. It's been nice having a pseudo-family step in for no reason other than they want me to be a part of things.

That relationship led to me moving here for school and getting insider information on this job when it came open and now… Nicole. Who I really am in love with despite my attempts to keep those feelings from developing. Still, that's my own personal business and I don't need Jaxon pushing the issue. And I certainly don't need to get fired when my boss finds out I have a hard-on for his soon-to-be sister-in-law.

I grab a bowl of pretzels knowing it's his preference and place it in front of him, avoiding eye contact. "I don't even really know her. Besides, she's related to the boss so she's off-limits. How are your clinics anyway? Do you get to do a bunch of cool stuff?"

"They're exhausting and I love it, but don't change the subject," he demands. "She is not off-limits because of Paul and don't try to feed me a bunch of horse shit on that. What's really going on?"

I shake my head dejectedly. I don't want to put my thoughts into words. He's only going to argue with me about the truth I already know and I'm not in the mood for that. Especially with her sitting just across the bar from us. Still, I know he isn't going to let it go. It seems to be a trait amongst the Hart family.

"I am a college student who hasn't declared a major yet and relied on his not-quite-brother to get him a job at a bar. I play video games for fun almost nightly and I'm not exactly sexy. She deserves way better than me. So, like I said, she's off-limits."

Jaxon's eyes soften and I want to roll mine at the pity I can see. Yet another reason I don't like talking about this kind of thing with him. What he thinks is self-deprecating talk is actually real to life. It doesn't hurt my feelings to know I'm not good enough for her. It is what it is. And what it is, is fact.

"Kade, you're a great guy—"

"Stop." I hold my hand up, shocked that he actually complies. "Listen, I know who I am and I'm fine with it.

I'm not trying to be anyone I'm not. Plus, Nicole doesn't need a date right now. She just needs a friend, right?"

Jaxon sighs in defeat. I'm sure this conversation isn't truly over, but I guess I've won this round. "You're right. A year sometimes feels like a long time but when you're healing from emotional wounds, it can take longer than that."

I know what he's referring to, even if I don't respond. I haven't asked for details, but from what I've been told Nicole ended up living in this area after her boyfriend beat the crap out of her. Just the thought of it makes me want to punch something even though I'd probably break my hand.

"Exactly. So let it go, will you?"

"For now," he concedes. It's as good as I'm going to get tonight.

I nod once. "Tell me about your clinicals. Have you removed any crowbars from anyone's thigh or done chest compressions while the gurney rolls down the hall?"

Jaxon snorts a laugh and grins. "You've been watching too many medical dramas."

I raise one shoulder quickly. "I learn some good information on those shows."

"On what shows?" Tammy drops her tray on the counter and looks at us expectantly. She's always interrupting, but no one minds. We're always surprised by what she contributes to any conversation. She's... entertaining.

"Kade seems to think he's practically a medical student because he likes to watch fictional doctor shows," Jaxon jokes.

Tammy doesn't seem to notice his sarcasm. "I'll tell you, I should have gotten my nursing license from how many episodes I've seen of House. Did you know I diagnosed my sister's husband's niece with an allergic reaction to the copper in her IUD because of Dr. Gregory House? And what do you know, when she finally took my advice and went to the doctor, I was right. They ripped that thing out of her so fast it'd make your head spin. Within days all that itching in her lady bits was gone. Of course, they ended up with another baby after that, but I suppose you can't always be rash and child free at the same time, can you?"

Jaxon and I stare at her blankly. I'm not sure if I'm not processing this conversation correctly or if Tammy truly is taking credit for someone else's unplanned pregnancy.

After a few seconds of awkward silence, she jumps back in.

"Got some orders for you when you're ready."

"Yeah now's a good time," I say quickly, praying she doesn't remember some other random story about the time she wasn't really a medical student and got way too into other people's business.

She prattles off the few drinks she needs and grabs a couple bowls of snacks to replenish the tables. As soon as she's out of earshot, Jaxon looks right at me. "Did she just tell us about some poor woman's lady bits?"

"I don't know. I got stuck on the visual of an IUD being flung across the room, man. Even if I wanted to date, I think I'm officially turned off from it forever."

Jaxon takes the final drink from his beer. "That was my cue to leave. She doesn't need to know anything about the toe fungus I had to irrigate today."

"Oh, come on!" I shout and throw my hands up in the air, making him laugh. "Did you need to give me that visual image, too?"

He pushes off the stool and tosses some bills on the counter. "That's the risk you take when you hang out with so many medical professionals."

He gives me some sort of a weird salute and takes off, leaving me shaking my head. I make a mental note to warn Nicole—no matter how much you may love Grey's Anatomy, don't ever bring it up in conversation with Tammy.

THREE
Nicole

"I'm coming, I'm coming!" I shout as I make my way toward the door, carrying the towel I'm using to dry my hands. I thought I had a few more minutes to finish up in the bathroom before they got here, but from the rattle of the doorknob, I guess not. Carson is one impatient kid these days.

Swinging the door open, I grab my nephew off the floor and hug him tightly to me, giving him kisses all over his sweet face and neck. He giggles and pulls me closer.

"I missed you, sweet boy," I coo.

"I missed you too, NicNic."

He's four now and can say my name with no problem, but I love that he still uses his nickname for me.

Releasing the tight grip I have on him, I push the dark hair out of his face. "I pulled out the box of Magic Tracks so we can make a giant road when your Mommy goes to work. How does that sound?"

"Yeah! I'm gonna make it all over the room!" He wriggles down, excited about working on his favorite activity while he's here. I'm not sure where the tracks came from, but we have a huge tote full of them and use every single one whenever he's here. It's not uncommon for his designs to stretch around the entire apartment. Even I have to admit it's pretty cool what this kid can make with these things.

Kiersten follows him in, giving me a quick hug as she lugs in his overnight bag.

"Thanks for watching him tonight."

"Of course I'm watching him." I shut the door and join her on the small couch where she's already ended up. "I understand why he spends time at Heath and Lauren's, but I am his aunt. I need my Carson fix, too, don't I buddy?" I lean over and grab him, smothering him with more kisses, much to his giggling delight.

"I know. Someday I'll get over the feeling that I'm inconveniencing everyone and just be grateful."

"Think of it this way—someday you'll have to return the favor to everyone else."

She nods thoughtfully. "Good point. But it better not be you any time soon."

"Ha!" I bark out loudly. "I'm sure you're really worried about that happening considering my recent hermit status."

Kiersten holds her hands up in mock defense. "I don't know who you bring home in the middle of the night. No judgment on my part."

"You're down the hall so you actually do know who I bring home every night. Besides, it's not you I'm worried about. There would be serious judgment from Paul and he can't afford to drive all his customers away with his overbearing brother act. So, in the best interest of him and his bar, I'll continue to stay here alone."

"You're such a good sister," Kiersten says with a giggle before her attention is diverted. "Hey what's this?"

I had forgotten I had a catalog from Southeast State sitting on my small coffee table.

"Just something I'm thinking about." And I have been. From the time I was a little girl, I wanted to go to college. When I finally made it, I was only there for a short time. I miss the atmosphere of classes and other students. These were supposed to be the most amazing four years of my life. I know I can't get it all back. Things are different now. But maybe I can at least get back into the classroom.

Kiersten picks it up and quickly flips through the pages with her thumb. "I'm kind of surprised they have these printed with the whole catalog being online."

"I requested it to be sent to me. I like having pages to hold. Things don't seem to translate as easily in my brain unless I can touch it."

"Oh yeah. I'm the same way." She tosses it back onto the table and turns to me. "Going back to school and a new job? That's a lot of big changes."

"I haven't done either yet. Baby steps, ya know?" I shrug like I'm indifferent, which I'm not. Not at all. Terrified is more like it, but the fear of staying stagnant for the rest of my life is somehow stronger than my fear of getting back out in the world so it's time to start trying.

"Well, you start working tomorrow so that's some good movement. And you know they have some of those partial semester classes that are only like three weeks or something."

"I saw that. I was thinking about trying that out first. They're pretty intense, a couple hours every single day for three straight weeks, but it might be a good way to see if I'm ready for something that requires a longer commitment."

"You've come so far." She taps her hand on my thigh in support. "I'm sure you're going to do just amazing."

"I hope."

We both look over when we hear a loud crash. Carson has apparently gotten tired of digging through the tote to find what he's looking for and has dumped the whole thing over. Pieces of the track slide everywhere and he immediately gets back to work building. Kiersten just shakes her head in amusement.

"I'm so glad he has a bunch of men in his life that can keep up with him. I'm not sure I have the energy half the time to be a boy mom."

"I don't know for sure since I haven't experienced it, but I bet it's just as hard being a girl mom," I retort. "Except instead of Magic Tracks you'd have paints everywhere and are stepping on those little tea party forks in the middle of the night. I bet those things hurt."

"You have a point. I'm already dreading the Lego phase that I'm sure is coming. Speaking of parenting though, guess who wants to come visit."

I furrow my brow. There's no way she's talking about our mother and yet I'm pretty positive she is.

"The woman who barely goes anywhere except shopping and to her country club wants to come here?" My sister nods, likely just as confused as I am about this situation. "Why?"

Kiersten shrugs. "She said something about wanting to have a relationship with her daughters. This, of course, was after she made a couple of digs about us never visiting her and how neglected she is by her own children."

"Of course."

Kiersten turns away as if gathering her thoughts on the matter. "I don't know what's going on with her. Maybe she's finally seeing the error of her ways or something."

I think on that assumption for a few minutes but it doesn't feel right. The last time I saw my mother was close to a year ago. She was the first person the police called when Jeremy put me in the hospital. They hadn't given her much information, just that I had been assaulted. When she first got there, she was the doting mother—asking questions about my injuries and prognoses, getting information about how best to help me recover—all those things someone who cares about you does.

And then I told her Jeremy had done it.

I will never forget the look on her face when the wall of indifference came down. My heart broke into a million pieces. Hearing your mother say she will not enable lies and turn her back on you while you lay literally bleeding and broken in a hospital bed was almost as hard as being beaten in the first place. Thank goodness for my sister who never once questioned my claims and gave me a safe place to live and a new start.

"I really don't think so, Kiersten. Maybe she just wants to butter us up so we'll take new family portraits that she can show off at the club."

Kiersten snorts a laugh. Not because it's funny, but because I'm probably right. "Don't ever let me treat Carson like that, okay?" She runs her hand over his hair lovingly as he snaps more tracks together.

"I don't think you could if you wanted to. Besides, that kid is attached to you like glue, still. He'd never let you leave him."

"Good point. We still have to let him fall asleep in our bed before moving him to his. And I still can't sleep naked because I never know if he's going to wake up in the middle of the night and climb back in with us."

"Stop doing that, Mama," Carson complains, clearly paying more attention to the conversation than we realized. "I sleep with you and Paul. That's our bed."

She raises her eyebrows at me in a look that screams, *"See what I mean?"* But being the good mom she is, she responds to him with, "I know, baby." It's a non-committal answer if I've ever heard one.

"Are you ready to start training tomorrow? I'm kind of excited about you working with us."

My heart leaps with a mixture of excitement and anxiety. "I am. It's time. I'm ready to stop relying on you guys and get back on my feet. I'm starting to feel, I don't know, like itchy just sitting around letting myself be taken care of."

"Well, this is a good first step."

"Do you know who's going to be training me tomorrow?"

"Paul is going to do tomorrow since he's the boss. But we'll rotate between him, me, and Kade as you go."

"Kade?" My heart stutters again, only this time it's knowing I'll be working so closely with the man I have a crush on. "I thought he was moving to the waiter position?" And I would have a little bit of distance so I don't accidentally put my feelings for him on display.

Thankfully Kiersten is oblivious to my minor distress. "Paul and I talked about it and the bar is at the point where we really need three people every night, not just during certain events. So Kade is going to do the same thing I do—waiter and bartend depending on what we need more each night. It'll kind of be like a flex role."

"Makes sense." And yet it still means I need to mentally prepare myself a bit more.

"And when we're not there, we're going to have him

step in as the manager on duty."

I feel a jolt of excitement for him. "Oooh… good for him."

"He's excited about it. Paul had already been considering it but the timing seems really good now."

"Anything I need to know to be ready for tomorrow?"

"Nope," she says as she pushes up from the couch and stretches out her back. "You've been around for long enough, you probably already know the most important parts. Like Dwayne's favorite drink and Frankie's favorite table."

That elicits a small laugh from me. The regulars are very predictable. "I'm most worried about using Paul's fancy new computerized system."

Kiersten's eyes light up at the mention of it. "Isn't it great? Don't get me wrong, I didn't mind the old register and having to stretch my short-term memory on orders, but it feels like we've finally entered the twenty-first century."

"Thank God I waited until now to start," I joke. "I prefer to work smarter, not harder. Are you leaving?"

"Yeah." She walks over to Carson who is already halfway across the room with his track and smooths down his hair before kissing the top of his head. "Since Paul and I are both here, I need to get Kade up to speed on prepping the front to open and his new management duties. I love you, Carson."

"Love you, Mama."

She turns for the door when Carson yells, "Mom! Wait!"

Jumping up from his spot, he runs to her and throws his arms around her legs, chin lifted and lips puckered, demanding a kiss. She smiles and complies.

"I love you sixty-five million three thousand!" he announces making me shake my head and stifle a smile.

"Still not understanding the Avengers reference, is he?"

"Nope," Kiersten replies. "But since I love him sixty-five million three thousand and one, it's fine with me."

"Oh man, mom, you win," Carson announces and walks her to the door, me following so I can lock it behind her.

As Kiersten leaves, he keeps his head poked out the door so he can continue to wave until she's down the hall and out of sight.

FOUR
Kade

"There's a guy up in the barn! He's in the loft window! Get him!"

Rodney is screaming through the headset until Matty finally takes down the bank robber we've been looking for. Of course, the rest of us didn't see him until after Archie was killed.

"Nice shot, Matty. Not that I'm surprised. How do you always get a shot off before I can even see him?" Seriously, this kid is easily the best *Red Dead Redemption* player I've ever met.

He's also the only *Red Dead Redemption* player I've met in person. Matty is Jaxon's actual biological brother and the person who got me hooked on this game. His dad hates it. Says Matty should be playing Madden games or something equally sports related. The rest of us just laugh about it. Jason Hart may have retired from football years ago, but his obsession continues and he has no problem trying to pass it off to his kids.

"It's just hand-eye coordination." Matty's voice crackles through the headset. "Coach is a stickler on that so I practice it every single day."

"Does he know it comes in handy while you're playing video games?"

Matty laughs. "As long as it means I'm knocking defenders out of the way, I don't think he gives a shit."

Along with being a fantastic gamer, Matty is proving to be an extremely talented football player. Not that anyone is surprised considering his Hall of Famer dad is a legend in the sport. The genes have definitely been passed on; Matty is the biggest seventeen-year-old kid I've ever seen in my life. I don't care for sports but at the few games I've been to, even I have been impressed with his talent. From what Jaxon tells me, colleges all over the country have been calling practically non-stop since last year trying to sweet-talk him into signing with their programs.

"Get outta the way! Get outta the way! He's got a shotgun!" Rodney yells and conversation stops as we all run for cover behind bales of hay.

"Where? Where do I look?" Archie jumps in, way behind all of us.

"Nice of you to join us again, Arch," I comment sarcastically.

"Give me a break. My mom wanted to talk about my day."

"Aw… did your mommy need some kisses from her baby…." Rodney chides and makes kissy noises.

"Shut the fuck up, man," is Archie's response. "She's cooking meatloaf tonight. I love that shit. I didn't want to piss her off or she'll screw it up."

"Oh yeah," Matty joins in. "Meatloaf always tastes better when it's made with looooooove…." he singsongs, eliciting a few choice words from Archie and laugher from the rest of us.

This is what I do with my afternoons off—play video games with a bunch of strangers and eat fast food. I've been told I need to get out more but I like my hobby. It's fun and I enjoy getting to know these guys. Besides, since I started working, I get a lot of social interaction so I'm not lacking in that department. It's almost weird how quickly I've been embraced by the whole staff and some of the customers simply because of my relationship with Jaxon. I'm not complaining. It's just odd to me how people can accept you, no questions asked, based on someone else's opinion.

Or maybe it's not weird and I'm still getting used to what others might call "normal" relationships.

Speaking of the bar, however…

"Okay y'all, I gotta jet," I say but continue playing. There's another bank robber out there and the reward is high for us to find him and turn him in.

They reply with a series of groans and "what the fuck, man?"

"Don't give me shit. Maybe you losers should start looking into jobs instead of giving me lip for doing mine. Might do you some good. Especially you, Archie. Eventually, you'll be able to move out of your mommy's house."

"Fuck you," he responds without much conviction behind his words.

"Jaxon told me Nicole is working there now."

My gun stops shooting when my thumb stumbles on the controller. Why the hell would Matty bring that up?

"Yeah? She started a week ago." I try for nonchalance. It's a good thing they can't see my face right now because I'm sure it's beet red.

"She's fucking gorgeous."

I feel myself getting defensive, even though I know there's no reason to feel that way. "Yeah, so?"

"So, I don't know how you can work around her without getting a hard-on."

Maybe there is a reason for me to feel defensive. "Easy. I'm not a misogynistic pig," I say with a little more venom than I intend. Unfortunately for me, Matty picks up on it.

"Why are you getting so mad? Do you like her?"

This time it's Archie's turn to make kissy sounds. I should have expected that. I may enjoy playing online with them, but I've never mistaken them for being the most mature bunch.

"Of course, I like her. She's a nice person and hopefully a good employee."

"Oh yeah. He's into her," Rodney says with a laugh.

I turn my avatar to his and shoot him in the foot.

"Dude! What the fuck!" he yells.

I flip the switch on my handset and toss it to the side. "I'm out, losers. Have fun diddling yourselves tonight."

They bid me farewell with a bunch of entertaining insults I only half hear as I shut everything down. My brain is already thinking about the night ahead of me. I've got eight hours of slinging drinks to focus on and more management duties to learn.

My small two-bedroom apartment isn't far from my work, only about a five-minute drive or so. It isn't until I'm inside the building and see Nicole behind the bar talking to Paul that I realize she must be working tonight.

Looking down at myself, I regret not wearing a nicer shirt. I immediately push that thought aside. I'm wearing a Frui Vita polo. It's standard for us most nights. And it doesn't matter what I wear. I not trying to impress Nicole anyway. There's no point.

"What's up?" I call out as I sidle up to our new touch screen monitor to clock in.

"Hey," Paul calls over his shoulder. "I'm training our new bartender today while you cover waiter duties."

Nicole gives me a quick, shy wave and I swear I fall a little more in love with her because of it. Or maybe it's just strong infatuation. Whatever you call it, I still have to clock in twice because her smiles throw me off guard enough I press all the wrong buttons the first time. In my defense, this is the first time we've been scheduled to work at the same time. Anyone would feel a little off-kilter when working with a new co-worker. Or so I tell myself.

"I'm glad you decided to work with us," I say to her, being one hundred percent honest just maybe not sharing my reasons. "Maybe that grumpy old man will chill out now."

Paul *harumphs* but I'm not looking at him. Nicole nods prettily and she's so damn beautiful, I have to force myself not to stare.

"Don't get excited yet." She tucks a strand of long blonde hair behind her ear. "It's still up in the air how good I am at this. I may be terrible and have to be fired."

"Not likely. You know how much Paul loves family. He'd rather close the bar than fire you."

"That's sweet of you to say but if I do that bad of a job, I'll quit."

"No one is quitting and no one is getting fired," Paul says and then points at me. "Except maybe you if you don't get this bar ready to open."

I snicker as I walk away. Paul is a great boss. Always kind and respectful. Gives people the freedom to make mistakes and learn the ropes. He not only pays fair wages, but goes beyond that when he can. The one thing that makes him prickly is Nicole. Not in a bad way. From what I understand, he just takes the big brother role seriously. No one is complaining, especially not me. I get it, I respect it and I appreciate it.

It doesn't take long to do a quick sweep of the floors to clear out anything that was missed last night and take all the chairs down from the tabletops. It gives me way too much time to sneak glances at Nicole as she follows Paul's instructions and learns to make some of our mixed drinks. She smiles the whole time, but that's just Nicole. Unless she's upset or in deep thought, her face naturally rests in a smile. Yet another thing I shouldn't notice about her because I should be keeping my distance, not allowing myself to be drawn in. It's like I'm asking myself to be heartbroken in the near future.

Soon enough the door is open for business. It's just a regular night tonight, no special events, so there's nothing extra that needs to be set up. It'll probably be a night of regulars.

As if on cue, the first one enters.

"Hey Dwayne, how's it going?"

"Good, good." He looks around the room, probably hoping to find his first victim, even though he beat them all here. As it turns out, Dwayne is a bit of a hustler. He's great at pool and any time he can convince someone to play him for money, it turns out in his favor. Most of the athletes that come in regularly have already figured Dwayne out, but he's such a nice guy, they still like the challenge of trying to beat him. Plus, they find it hilarious when they can help Dwayne hustle a rookie. It boosts team morale or something. That's probably the only reason Paul still allows Dwayne to do it.

"I haven't seen Jimmy around lately," I mention casually, only slightly concerned we haven't seen Dwayne's sidekick in a while.

"He got himself a new job working nights at some distribution center."

I whistle low through my teeth. "I hear you can make some good money doing that. Especially during the overnight hours."

"You can make better money hustling the pros at pool, though." He winks at me and I can't help but laugh.

"Sounds a lot more fun, too," I joke back. "Does that mean you're sticking with water tonight or you wanna start with something harder?"

Dwayne takes a seat at the table closest to the pool table, staking his claim, and stretches out his jean-clad legs. "I think I'm in the mood for one of those Apple Pie ales. Once we see who comes in tonight, I'll decide if I need to switch to water."

"Sounds like a plan. I'll be back."

I head back up to the bar to place his order and start off what will hopefully be a busy night. I'll need it if I want to focus on anything but Nicole and how her long lashes brush against her cheek when she blinks. It's the curse of having her work here yet I wouldn't have it any other way.

FIVE

Nicole

I stare at myself in the mirror as I finish wave ironing the last section of my hair. My makeup is flawless except for that one zit on my chin. My outfit is a simple pair of skinny jeans with comfy boots and a Frui Vita t-shirt because I couldn't decide what else to wear.

I've been training as a bartender for a couple of weeks now so I'm fairly confident in what I'm doing, but this is the first time I've been nervous to go in. Of course, tonight is also the first night Paul and Kiersten think I'm ready to go at it without their assistance, so I'll be working solo with Kade. I can't seem to keep the nerves at bay.

I'm not afraid of doing the job wrong. I know there are minor problems I'll run into, but that's not the issue. I'm nervous about being so close to Kade.

In the last couple of weeks as I've gotten to know him, I've realized what a kind and gentle person he is. Not one to be the life of the party, he's just… steady. Calm. Practically unflappable. And don't get me started on how in tune he is with the customers.

Just the other day, he was the first to notice one of the female patrons acting like she felt uncomfortable. I watched as he discreetly approached her and within minutes, he walked her outside to a waiting Uber and safely away from the guy that was giving her a bad vibe.

I asked him about it later and he brushed it off like it was something anyone would do. I know firsthand that is unequivocally not true. And then I swooned. Hard.

Up until that point, I'd been able to write him off as "just another guy" who puts his best foot forward when he's in public, but I no longer think that's it. I'm almost positive with Kade, what you see is what you get. Therein lies the problem.

Kade is now starring in my silliest, most cheesy romantic fantasies and while I know it's okay, everyone does it, I feel foolish for putting him up on a pedestal. That'll make the crash harder if he turns out not to be everything I imagine he is. And yet, somehow, I already know that won't happen.

Maybe even worse, I'm afraid he'll see right through me and know immediately that I have feelings for him. He's never given me any indication he feels the same way and I would never want to make our work environment uncomfortable because of my silly, unrequited crush. I just have to make sure to keep my eyes on my job and off him and his mop of dark hair that always seems disheveled, even though I like it that way. It makes him perfectly imperfect.

Doing a last-minute glance over my hair to make sure I didn't miss any strands, I take a deep, cleansing breath.

Breathe in, two, three, four… hold, two, three, four… and out, two, three, four… and hold.

It doesn't actually cleanse anything, but at least it

makes my heart slow down just a touch.

I do a quick spritz of my favorite scent, grab my keys, and head out the door, making sure it's locked behind me.

The benefit of living in the small apartment behind the bar is it's a ten-second walk to work so it's almost impossible to be late. Being that I'm still technically in training, Kade is already here and prepping to open when I slide behind the counter.

"Hi," I greet him hoping my voice isn't shaky from nerves. I keep my eyes diverted as I touch the monitor that's mainly used to take orders and run tabs, but also has a function where we can clock in. My fingers are shaking just enough it takes me a couple of tries to get my employee ID number right.

"Hey." He gives me a glance up and down and I almost shiver even though we aren't making any physical contact. "You look nice."

"Oh." I look down at my uniform shirt and smooth it down a bit. "I had a hard time deciding what to wear so I just went with the easy option."

"I didn't mean the outfit. I just mean you."

"Oh."

That did nothing to help the situation with my nerves at all. If I'm not mistaken, Kade may have a bit of a blush on his cheeks as well. I hope he doesn't think he crossed a professional line or something.

When I don't say anything else, Kade clears his throat and turns back to what he's doing.

"Paul wants you to do as much as you can on your own. I'm just here to help you out if you get stuck and to pick up the slack when it gets busy. Will that work for you?"

"Sure. I'm kind of excited to be doing it on my own at this point. Where do you want me to begin?"

"There's not much left to do. I've already emptied the dishwasher and made sure the shelves are stocked so we have enough liquor on hand. The till is ready to go and Tammy will be here in a few minutes to get the front ready. All we need to do is fill the bowls with peanuts and pretzels and cut up the citrus fruit. Do you have a preference on which one you want to do?"

I really don't. "Um, I'm right by the fridge so I might as well start working on the fruit."

"Sounds like a plan."

The silence is palpable as I finish with the touch screen and we both get started on our tasks. I keep trying to come up with something to say, some conversation starter, but I'm drawing blanks. We already know surface level stuff about each other like where we're from and who our families are so small talk is out. We could discuss the weather but it's central Texas. It's hot and humid like every other September day.

Finally, Tammy walks in the door and I breathe a sigh of relief. If I'm not mistaken, Kade does too. But if anyone can break the awkwardness, it's her.

"Howdy kids! How's it hanging?" Like I said, Tammy is never short on words.

"Good," Kade calls back. "You ready for tonight?"

"I'm always ready for this place to be hopping." She heads toward the monitor to clock in and frowns as she looks at the screen, but that doesn't stop her from conversing. "Nothing makes me happier than knowing we can let those boys come here and have a good time. And what in the hell am I doing wrong with this computer thingy? Kade?"

I hide my smirk behind my hair. There is a reason Tammy still places orders the old fashioned way—by shouting them out to us. She can never figure out how the touch screen works and we're all pretty resigned to the fact that she probably never will.

"I got it," Kade says with a smile and my heart melts when he has to push his black-rimmed glasses up his nose. Not everyone would take Tammy's inability to use the new system in stride, but that's just Kade. He won't hold it against her and he never gets annoyed by having to help with the smallest task.

"You're a good man, Kade Maxwell." Tammy pats his arm kindly. "If I had a son, I'd want him to be just like you."

"That's really nice of you, Tammy, thanks."

The blush on his cheeks is back. That seems to happen whenever he gets a compliment and I get the distinct impression he doesn't get many, which makes me sad. He's such a good person he should be showered with accolades often.

Kade turns back to me as Tammy begins to set up for the night.

"How's it going with the limes?"

"I'm almost done."

"Cool."

He goes back to the peanuts and the silence settles over us once again. I want to kick myself for having no idea how to talk to Kade. It's not like I have trouble making conversation. But with him, I just seem to freeze up.

I'm not the only one who seems to notice the quietude and wonder how to fix it.

"What the hell is going on back there?" Tammy slides behind the bar and grabs a clean tray, setting it on the counter. "Are you two fighting?"

Kade and I look at each other and shrug.

"No," he finally says. "We're just prepping for tonight."

Snatching a clean apron off the shelf, Tammy wraps it around her waist. "It's the most quiet this place has ever been. I get that you're here to work but loosen up, kids! Don't be such Debbie Downers."

My lips quirk up on the side as I place the container of freshly cut lime wedges in the fridge and grab some oranges.

"Don't worry Tammy," I jest playfully. "We'll do better to keep you entertained. I'll try not to concentrate so hard on working."

"Good. People don't like feeling awkward when they're out for drinks. Awkward feeling people don't tip well." She points her finger back and forth at us. "Don't make me lose out on tips because you two can't figure out a little sexual tension."

My eyes widen and Kade makes a choking sound at her shocking accusation. How did she know I had a crush on Kade? And how am I supposed to work with him now that she blew the lid of my tightly held emotions?

"We don't… we can't…" Kade stutters over his words, unable to make a complete sentence. I can't even put words together so he's doing better than me.

"Oh, pish posh." Tammy waves her hand like we're being ridiculous, which we probably are but she just made it a hundred times more uncomfortable. "A little sexual tension and flirting never hurt anyone. You are two grown-ass adults. Figure it out and have a little fun while you work together. I guarantee time will go by faster and this here tip jar," she clunks it down on the counter, "will fill up faster because of it."

She takes off again, leaving Kade and I to bumble our way through a forced conversation.

"That uh, that wasn't really necessary of her." Kade shoves his hands in his pockets, looking everywhere but at me. Not that I blame him. I'm sure he's uncomfortable now that my crush has been called out.

"I hope it doesn't make working with me uncomfortable."

"As long as we remain professional, I don't think it will be a problem."

Professional. If I ever wondered about how Kade feels about me, I guess I have my answer.

"Of course." I force a smile that I hope he can't tell is fake. "We'll just pretend Tammy never said that."

Kade nods once, gives me a quick smile and goes back to his work. We still don't make conversation. Awkward turned into uncomfortable for everyone so there's not much we can do to fix it at this point. We don't have to try for long, though. As expected, the place is full of customers within a couple of hours.

I'm pretty pleased with myself for keeping up as well as I do, even when Tammy comes rushing up to give me a bunch of orders I have to remember in detail.

"I need two buckets of long necks, a whiskey sour, one whiskey neat, and a bottled water for our old pal Dwayne who is apparently hustling a rookie tonight at the insistence of his team."

I snicker and grab the buckets since they're already prepped and ready to go. "What team is that anyway?"

When they first came in, I assumed it was the local basketball team judging by their collective heights. But these days with so many various teams coming in, I've learned it's always best to ask.

"Which table?" Tammy rests against the bar. "We've got one table full of basketball players and another of hockey players. All very rich, very attractive, and very single." She wiggles her eyebrows at me in suggestion.

"I didn't realize you were on the prowl tonight, Tammy," I joke and grab the whiskey off the shelf.

"Not for me, you doofus. For you. It's been how many months since you got away from your jackass of an ex-boyfriend?"

I wince at the reminder. The one bad thing about this being a family-owned and operated business is how many people get in mine sometimes.

"It's time for you to cozy on up to a new fella." Tammy leans in as if to tell me a secret. "Nothing says revenge against an ex more than dating someone a thousand times better than they ever were and those two tables are full of men that meet that expectation."

I swallow my laughter and place the final two drinks on her tray. "Thank you for your suggestion. How about I get through my training period first before I start hitting on the customers."

She shrugs and picks up the tray of drinks, securing it in her arms. "It's your life. Just don't wait too long or those young hotties will be snatched up by someone else."

"Noted," I call after her as she walks away.

First, Tammy's calling out my crush on Kade and telling us to do something about it. Now she's trying to get me to hook up with a customer. I rarely understand Tammy, but at least she's entertaining.

"What was that about?" Kade asks as he grabs some liquor from the shelf. He's been doing double duty as bartender and waiter tonight. Makes me feel good to know I'm doing a good enough job he feels comfortable leaving me alone behind here sometimes.

"Oh, just Tammy being Tammy. Trying to hook me up

with a customer."

Kade gets a hardened look on his face. "You know Paul doesn't allow that right?"

It takes me a few seconds to respond, taken aback that Kade would assume I'd ever do anything like that. "I know. I'd…I'd never."

He inspects me for a few seconds, likely looking to see if I'm lying. I don't like the way it feels, but I also understand it. He's worked with so many employees that have quit in the last six months. I'm sure he's just worried I'm going to get myself fired before things can finally settle down a bit.

"Really, Kade," I reiterate. "I don't have any interest in these guys. They're nice and all, but I'm not interested in dating an athlete."

That seems to take the edge off whatever he's feeling. Or at least I hope that's why he goes back to making his drinks.

I don't have time to think about it though. I have a customer to serve first.

"Hi, what can I get you?" I say with a smile.

The man pushes his floppy blond hair out of his face. I recognize him. He was here for Trivia Night a few weeks ago and wore an ugly green shirt. If I remember correctly, he's a member of the San Antonio Slingers hockey team.

Leaning against the counter, he settles in and I already know what's coming before he says a word.

"For starters, your phone number, beautiful."

I can't help it. He's trying so hard to give me swoony eyes and failing so miserably, I laugh. Loudly. "Does that line ever work?"

The flirtation comes to a screeching halt and he pushes his hair back again. "It never has so far. And yet I still keep trying."

I like that he has a sense of humor. Makes things a little less difficult after turning him down.

"I'm sure it will someday. But unfortunately, my number isn't on the menu. I can make you a drink, though."

He drops down on a stool and I have a feeling he's going to stay awhile. I don't mind. I kind of enjoy when our customers are chatty. Makes me feel like I'm pulling out of my shell a bit.

"I'll just have a long neck for now."

"Coming right up."

It takes just a few seconds to grab his beer and pop the top off, handing it to him.

"Do you already have a tab going?"

"Yeah. Tucker Hayes."

I quickly add his beer to his tab and turn back around to see he hasn't returned to his friends. He's still sitting at the bar watching whatever game is on behind me. I never really pay much attention to the televisions here. Even when I'm not working, people-watching is so much more fun.

"You're Nicole, right?"

"Sure am. And you're Tucker Hayes. I assume you're one of the Slingers?"

He gives me a grin, like he's thrilled I know this about him. Unfortunately for him, I only know because of Trivia Night, not because I've done any research.

"I am."

"Aren't you guys in the middle of pre-season? Should you be drinking tonight?"

Tucker chuckles and takes another swig. "We go in a little late tomorrow so most of us just decided to come out and relax. Is that okay with you?"

He may not be hitting on me anymore, but he's definitely still flirty.

"Just let me know if you need me to cut you off at a certain point. I'd hate for you to have to skate around with a hangover. That sounds terrible actually, now that I think about it."

"I'll be out of your hair long before you have to intervene, I promise. But do you mind if I just hang here for a bit?" He gestures over his shoulder. "I see those losers every day. I could use a little less guy talk for a bit."

"Sure. Just let me know if you need anything."

He gives me a quick wink and I turn back to the computer to see what orders have come in. Before I can grab what I need, Kade sidles up next to me.

"You sure Tammy isn't onto something? Pretty sure Tucker Hayes just hit on you."

I'm not sure why Kade is so concerned but I don't want him to worry. The wink I just got did absolutely nothing for me, which makes part of me wonder if I'm broken, but I assume it's only because I'm half in love with the guy standing next to me.

"I'm pretty sure Tucker Hayes hits on a lot of people. I'm not interested. But if a little conversation means he goes home happy tonight, I'll be fine. Besides, remember what Tammy said about tips."

We both turn just as Tucker slides what appears to be a ten-dollar bill in the tip jar.

I raise an eyebrow at Kade who nods, understanding my point, then joins me in mixing.

I spend the rest of the evening with steady orders, fun conversation, and thanking the heavens that the awkwardness finally seems to have dissipated a bit. Fingers crossed it stays that way.

SIX
Kade

hate morning classes. Not that being here at eleven is early. I just prefer afternoons because of how late I work most nights. It's hard enough to stay awake during my Economics class without the added issue of being tired. I barely made it through today's lecture because I just find it all so boring. I swear it was the longest hour and a half of my life.

I would have taken a different class but I've been avoiding my mandatory Economics credits for so long I ran out of options and finally had to suck it up. The only good thing about suffering through is at least it helps eliminate one degree option. With the way I'm struggling, it's obvious that business is out. Now, if I could only figure out what my major should be, it would give me a little more room to play with in my schedule, but I honestly have no idea what I want to do with my life. I'm also a tiny bit terrified that I'll pick the wrong career path and end up stuck in a dead-end job that I hate.

I'm toying with computer science or even computer

programming because I think it would be fun to design video games. But I also know how difficult it is to get a job in that industry. Plus, enjoying *playing* video games doesn't mean I would enjoy *making* them.

Thankfully, I've still got a couple of semesters to figure it out. If I can. I'm not holding out a lot of hope at this point.

I sigh deeply as I wander across campus. All those career tests they made us take in high school didn't help one bit when it comes to figuring this stuff out. I suppose working at the bar isn't the worst job to have while I sort through it all. Speaking of the bar…

Is that Nicole? And why does she look lost? Do I help her? I can't just leave her alone to try to find wherever she's going. That would just be a dick move.

Decision made, I do a quick breath check in my hand before approaching her.

"Nicole, hey."

Her face immediately brightens when she sees me and I can't help but smile back at her. She's so damn beautiful when she smiles. Well, she's beautiful all the time but this look is my favorite.

"Hi, Kade. How are you?"

"A little overwhelmed with my Economics class and not looking forward to my next exam, to be honest."

"That doesn't sound encouraging." She looks down at what appears to be a course catalog in her hand. "I was hoping to sign up for that class."

"You're going back to school?"

Nicole blushes prettily and I know I've embarrassed her. I hope it's not because I reminded her of how she dropped out. It's not a well-kept secret a Frui Vita that her ex-boyfriend beat her so badly she ended up in the hospital and that's why she quit school. From what I've been told, she didn't leave Kiersten's side for a long time, even while her sister was working. Even with her bruises on full display, Nicole stayed glued to her favorite stool with her back against the wall. Or so I've been told. Luckily, I never saw the marks.

I've only picked up bits and pieces of conversations about the situation, but the regular patrons seem to have put two and two together and now it's an unspoken rule that no one messes with Nicole. Unless you are having a normal, platonic conversation with her, she's off-limits until she says otherwise. So far, I haven't seen any indication that's she's done that yet. Not even with that fucker Tucker Hayes who tried to move in on her the other night.

"I'm trying to sign up but the campus is so big." She looks around the grassy area, obviously overwhelmed. "I'm having a hard time finding the registrar's office."

"It's just in the administration building. I can walk you over there if you like." An idea hits me and I take advantage of it before I chicken out. "Or would you like to join me for lunch first? I was going to the snack bar for food. Their soup and sandwich combo is actually pretty good and a lot cheaper than the deli down the street."

Her eyes look down at the sidewalk briefly before she peeks up at me through her lashes. "I'd like that."

Her reaction confuses me. She almost seems nervous to be around me. Is it because of Tammy and her big mouth? I don't want Nicole to feel awkward. I want her to feel comfortable. To know I'd never hurt her, not ever, and I'd never push her for something more than friendship if she didn't want it. So, I make a point of keeping enough room in between us as I walk next to her.

"It's right over here." I point out the building I was

headed toward so we can stroll that way.

"How come you don't like your Economics class?" she asks after a few seconds of awkward silence. "Is the professor really hard or something?"

I don't want to tell her the truth—that I'm a loser who can't get his shit together. But after our initial awkward silence when she started working, I've discovered she's also really easy to talk to. And even though Tammy blew my cover and basically put my feelings on a giant neon sign in front of the one person I didn't want to know about my unrequited crush, Nicole isn't treating me any differently. I guess there's no harm in telling the person who friend-zoned you what your deal is.

"It's just boring to me. I don't really care about capital goods versus industrial goods versus essential goods. There is so much more math involved and it's not like regular math. It's economics math."

Nicole giggles. "That doesn't even make sense."

"Exactly." I hike my backpack up a little further as we walk and I grumble, "At least I know I probably don't want to be a business major," trying to keep myself in a positive mindset but I'm not sure it's working.

"What *do* you want to do?"

Isn't that the million-dollar question? "I have no idea. It seemed like a good idea, starting college without any direction. I don't have to decide on a major for the first two years so I figured I'd try it out and see if I got any clarity. But all I can see is the deadline to declare looming in the distance. I'll probably end up working at the bar for the rest of my life."

"There's no shame in working there forever," she says kindly and it makes me love her all the more. Or like. Or crush. Hell, I don't even know. The last time I had feelings remotely close to this, I was in high school and crushing on a girl named Melissa. This feels so much more intense than that.

"We'll see." I know it's a non-answer, but I need to quit with the pity party. I'm taking the girl of my dreams out to lunch. I should be on cloud nine right now. "This is the place," I say changing subjects and pull the door open for her to walk in.

We get in line and Nicole's eyes take in the small, café-like area. There are the standard open coolers for pre-made food and snacks, and a large fridge full of bottled drinks. One of the counters is set up with a clear sneeze guard you can see through as you decide if you want soup and which one. Behind that is where several students in the work program do all the cooking. They serve everything from fried cheese to pizza to burgers and nachos. I'm surprised it's not busier this time of day. Then again, it is almost one. The lunch crowd is probably just thinning out.

"You said soup and sandwich, right?"

"If that's what you're craving. The whole menu is on that giant chalkboard except for the pre-made food."

Nicole looks around and I swear she hasn't stopped smiling since we walked in.

"I guess this will do for you?"

"What?" She looks at me blankly before her thoughts catch up with her. "Oh. Sorry. Yes."

I furrow my brow. "What are you thinking?"

"Just about how nice it is to be back on campus. I mean, I don't go here yet or anything, but I really love college. I love the vibe and the people and things like this—a random café where I can get anything I want to eat at whatever time of day. I miss it."

"So, you're into learning?"

She twists her lips and thinks for a moment. "I like new experiences. I don't mind the learning, but college life is so much more than just learning in the classroom. Does that sound strange?"

I shake my head because it doesn't. At all. If anything, it makes me more intrigued. I keep that thought to myself, though.

"Then it's a good thing you're going back."

"Yeah," she says quietly and looks back at me. "Yeah, I think you're right. Thank you for bringing me here, Kade. This is just what I needed today."

My chest swells with unnecessary pride. I'm not the one cooking. "I hope their food lives up to your expectations."

"Next!" the cashier yells. I guess we'll find out soon enough.

I order my normal baked potato soup with a turkey melt sandwich and side of fried pickles, because everyone should *always* get fried pickles. Nicole goes with all the unhealthy food—chicken tenders, fries, and a side of fried cheese. I like that she didn't pick a salad. She, on the other hand, does not like when I pay for both our lunches.

"No, Kade!" She tries to snatch my credit card away but it's too late. It's already in the machine. "I know how much you make and you need to save your money."

"You also know I recently got a small raise at work and how tips are going lately, so you know one lunch isn't going to kill my budget." Not that I really have one. I don't exactly have a hopping social life.

She finally gives up on her resistance when the card machine beeps and she realizes there's no going back now. "Well thank you. That was really nice of you."

"It's not a problem." I can feel myself getting uncomfortable with her compliment so I go for distraction. "Where would you like to sit?"

"Um, can we find a spot by the window? I like people watching."

"I knew that about you." I guide her through the maze of tables to find what she's looking for. "You did a lot of sitting and observing in your spot at the bar."

Nicole makes a quick detour to grab some napkins and utensils from the small counter while we chat. "I didn't know anyone noticed."

"Oh, I noticed." I grimace and tilt my chin down. Just when we were finally getting past the awkwardness, I go and say something like that. "I mean, it's hard not to notice when someone is there every night. You were kind of like a regular."

Done. I think I saved myself. At least I hope I did. Nicole doesn't seem to have any physical reaction to my faux pas and she hasn't run away screaming so I think I'm good.

"It worked in my favor though." She slides into a chair at a small table right next to the large window. "I already knew half the customers when I started and what their drink of choice is."

"This is true." Slinging my backpack over my chair, I join her. "Not that it's hard to remember Dwayne is either going to drink water or an Apple Pie ale."

"Yeah, that one is pretty easy." She takes a breath, and that awkward silence is back. I hate this part. I don't typically have problems conversing with people, although I don't go out of my way to talk to just anyone. But Nicole is different and consequently, I'm overthinking. I just don't want to say anything wrong when I'm with her. The crazy part is, I don't even know what wrong would be. I just know I don't want to do it.

At least we can stick to one topic while we wait for our food.

"Since the semester already started, how are you going to register for classes?"

I swear Nicole breathes a sigh of relief at the topic change. I can't help but wonder if that means she's feeling the same anxiety I am. Which would be weird since she's just about perfect and I can't think of anything she could say that would sound strange to me.

"I'm not sure I'm totally ready for this much, I don't know… time in public I guess. Working is one thing. I'm comfortable there. But being here? Let's just say it took me a couple hours to get enough nerve to come to campus by myself."

That makes me sad for her. And yet, I admire how strong she is. She powered through and accomplished her goal. There's something to be said for that.

"How do you feel now that you're here?"

She thinks for a moment before answering. "Proud of myself, for one."

"As you should be."

Nicole flashes me a quick smile and continues. "I think I'm ready. Maybe. They have a few of those rapid evening classes I want to try. It's like an entire semester's worth of class squeezed into three weeks. I figure if I can make it through that with no issue, I can consider taking a regular class or two next semester."

"Can I just make one suggestion?" I offer. She nods in response. "If you can get into that rapid Economics class, do it. It'll suck but three days a week I spend an hour and a half wishing to get the flu or something so I don't have to be there."

Nicole giggles and it's possibly the most attractive

sound I've ever heard. "I'll do just that, thank you."

Our food finally arrives and we spend the rest of our time eating instead of talking. But this time the silence isn't awkward at all, it's comfortable. I like it. It seems we've come a long way already.

SEVEN
Nicole

"**I** took the liberty of calling you lovely ladies an Uber and it's waiting for you. You ready to go?"

I strain my ears to listen as Kade navigates his way through an awkward conversation with a bunch of drunk bridesmaids who've had way too much to drink tonight. Or at least I assume they're bridesmaids. The t-shirts that have the words "I'm with the bride" written in a very strategic location across their chests were the first indicator they came here for a bachelorette party.

The second indicator was the massive amount of shots they ordered and consumed.

"You're so cute," one particularly cute bridesmaid slurs as she runs her finger down Kade's chest. "You're like a big teddy bear. I just wanna cuddle you."

Having lost all her inhibitions, she wraps her arms around his midsection and tries to settle in. I wonder if she's right about what it's like to hug him. I hate that she's finding out but I'm not.

I continue to take glances up while I work, watching as

Kade quickly, yet gently removes her arms from him and helps her steady herself on her own two feet.

"Thank you, you're sweet. Let's get you guys out of here."

"I have my car. But where are my keys?" someone else asks and begins digging through her purse. She finds what she's looking for and holds them up in the air. "Here they is… are… is? What's the word?"

Kade gently pulls the keys from her hand. "Thank you for finding these for me." She looks at him, confused and likely having already forgotten what they were talking about. "I'll keep these for you until tomorrow and then you can come get them."

"But what will I do with my car?" She hiccups right in his face. He doesn't even flinch.

"I'm going to take care of it for you."

"But I can drive," she tries unsuccessfully to argue.

"But I would feel so sad if something happened to you. And I want you to get home safe so you can come back another day."

A huge smile breaks out on the bridesmaid's face and suddenly all the women are following Kade outside, telling him how much fun they had and how nice he is. He just keeps it moving, never once getting annoyed or upset by the extra effort, and likely forgotten tips.

Lots of men pretend to care about the well-being of others, but I've never known anyone like Kade who just does it without a second thought.

It's so sexy.

"Hey," Kiersten says as she eases up next to me and grabs a bucket of long necks. "What's got you so deep in thought tonight?"

I could tell her I've been eavesdropping on our co-worker, but I'm not going to. She'd just interfere and my growing attraction to Kade is one thing I need to figure out on my own. So, I lie.

"Nothing. Just feeling kind of mellow. How is my wonderful nephew anyway?"

"Oh, I didn't tell you!" She leans against the shelves to settle in. This must be good. "The other day Carson asked if Paul was his daddy."

My eyes widen in shock. The issue of Carson's parentage is a hard one to discuss with a four-year-old. How do you say "Well, your daddy died before you were born, but it turns out he was living a double life and wasn't the nicest of men"? You don't. You sort of sit back and wait for him to ask questions and hope you can come up with a good answer on the fly.

I grip her arm. "And? What did you say?"

"I asked if he wanted Paul to be his daddy and when he nodded, Paul almost burst into tears."

I put my hands over my heart. I can't help it. It might explode from all the sweetness.

"So, from here on out," she continues, "Paul is Carson's daddy and no one can tell him otherwise."

"Kiersten that is so amazing."

She nods sweetly. "It really is. It's just hard to wrap my mind around the fact that two years ago, I had resigned myself to raising him all alone and just did my best to surround him with good people who loved him. And now here we are, with Carson getting the best dad ever."

"You know this means you need to start working on number two, right?"

She rears back like I've slapped her. "Hell no. Carson is enough of a handful. Let's wait until he's sleeping in his own bed first before we talk about adding another to the mix."

I'll give her that, even though it probably means I won't have another niece or nephew to spoil until Carson is a teenager.

Chuckling to myself, I turn to greet the customer that just sat down. "Hi, what can I get… Mom?"

"Hello, Nicole."

It feels almost like an out-of-body experience seeing her here. The last time I saw my mother was when she left me at the hospital over a year ago. We've talked on the phone, mostly about gossip and her country club and other shallow things, but there's definitely a rift between us.

"Wha-what are you doing here?"

She completes her assessment of the bar and is obviously unimpressed. "Since my daughters never come to see me, I thought I'd take time out of my schedule to come see them at this… establishment… instead."

I want to yell at her that the last time I saw her, she was kicking me while I was down. But she's my mom and I'm not sure how to stand up for myself without being disrespectful. And maybe there's still a tiny bit of hope that she's here to apologize.

"It's a long drive. Can I get you something to drink?"

"You wouldn't happen to have a white wine spritzer do you?"

"Not that I've ever seen. But I do have white wine."

She huffs, probably irritated with the nervous shakiness in my hands from seeing her. I could say I don't care, but that's untrue. Is she sorry she left me at my lowest point? Does she believe me now? Does she want to fix things between us? A million thoughts run through my mind.

"I guess that'll do."

I grab the chardonnay out of the fridge and grab a wine

glass to begin pouring. Thank goodness Kiersten finally notices mom at this point because I'm at a loss as to what to do next.

With a saccharine sweet smile on her face, Kiersten leans on the counter and rests her chin on her fist. "Mom. What brings you here a week early?"

Our mother practically sneers at her, their relationship tumultuous at best. "Honestly Kiersten, do you have to be so rude?"

"That depends on the answer to my question," Kiersten responds without batting an eyelash. I just quietly place the drink in front of our mother and back away, letting them hash this out.

Mom responds by taking a sip of her wine, clearly making my sister wait for an answer. This is the game they've played with each other for years. Or at least since Kiersten stopped trying to make her happy and went about her life without worrying about parental approval. Me? I haven't gotten to that point yet. I'm still hoping to have a better relationship with her.

Placing the glass back on the counter, Mom finally answers Kiersten.

"I was going to be here next week but plans changed when Jeremy informed me he was coming this way and offered me a ride to the hotel."

Jeremy? My Jeremy? Er, my EX Jeremy? There's no way.

My heart begins to race as I watch my biggest nightmare begin to unfold before my eyes.

"I suggested we stop here first on the off chance either of you is working and so here I am. With both of you."

The door opens and he walks in, all swagger and money, like he doesn't have a care in the world. Every step he takes closer to the bar is another step backward I take until I have nowhere else to go. I'm right up against the shelves staring at the man who claimed he loved me and then used his fists to prove he was a liar.

Kiersten turns to see me backed up in panic, likely sporting a terrified look on my face. "That's him, isn't it?"

It takes everything in me to nod. I don't even think I'm breathing anymore. That, combined with my heart racing with adrenaline and I think I'm going to pass out. *What is he doing here? How did he find me? Did she tell him where I was? Is he going to come after me again?*

I feel like a cornered animal, with nothing but the anticipation of his fist in my face to keep me company.

Kiersten immediately whips back around to confront our mom. "How dare you bring him here? He is not welcome."

My mother barely blinks, completely unflappable by Kiersten's tone. "I have spoken to Jeremy at length and he assures me none of what Nicole said is true. But he loves her so much he wanted to come and work out their misunderstanding."

"Misunderstanding?" Kiersten roars. "Did you even see the bruises? Did you get the hospital bill?"

"I did, but I refused to pay it. I won't condone lies like that."

They continue to argue but my eyes are on Jeremy. He's smiling at me. To anyone else, it would look sincere. But I've seen that look before and it's anything but genuine. He knows exactly what he's doing by being here. He may have lost me, but he's making sure I know he hasn't lost *control* of me. That he will come in and out of my life however he wants and will even sacrifice the last of my relationship with my mother to do it.

My hands continue to shake and I grab a random cork-screw off the counter, holding it in front of me. It's not much of a weapon but right now I have no idea what else to do. He was ballsy enough to show his face here, will he be ballsy enough to try to get over the counter to me? I just don't know. I don't know anything right now except terror.

Kiersten continues to rant and it looks like her head might explode at any moment. "You need to leave," she finally yells, completely ignoring the fact that our customers all seem to be paying attention to the commotion now. "Get out. Now. Both of you."

Jeremy takes a step forward but Kade, who I didn't notice before, moves to the front of the bar, blocking his line of sight. "You may have noticed the sign that says we reserve the right to refuse service to anyone." Kade's voice is strong and steady. "We've never had to enforce that rule, but there's a first time for everything. Tonight is the night. Please leave."

My eyes dart back and forth between my mother's face and Kade's back. I've never heard him say anything but kind words so he must be really angry. For whatever rea-son, it makes me feel the tiniest bit more calm. I know he's several inches shorter than my ex-boyfriend and he doesn't work out, but somehow, I feel like Kade would fight to the death for me.

Jeremy tries to move to the side, but Kade steps the same way, blocking him again.

"Well, I have never been treated so poorly in my life," mom says, using a carefully calculated tone. "You better believe I'll be speaking with your boss."

"You mean my live-in boyfriend?" Kiersten sneers. "Don't worry. I'll be talking to him first since he helped me pick up the pieces last time you let that monster hurt her."

Mom stands abruptly and smooths down her clothing, head held high. "I am so disappointed. In the both of you." She says that last part holding my gaze and I know in that moment, my relationship with my mother is officially over.

They both turn, but not before Jeremy is able to make eye contact one final time, ensuring I know this isn't over. Then I watch their backs as they head out the door.

It's only when it latches shut that I lose my ability to stand up. The corkscrew clatters to the floor and I slide down the wall, landing on my rear. I can hear my gasps of breath as I try to get some oxygen in my lungs. It doesn't seem to be working.

Jeremy is back.

Jeremy is back.

Jeremy is never going to leave me alone.

Kiersten is immediately at my side. "Nicole. I got you. They're gone. Can you breathe with me?"

I shake my head, eyes wide with terror.

"Yes, you can. Follow me. Breathe in, two, three, four… hold, two, three, four… breathe out, two, three, four… hold, two, three, four."

We do the breathing sequence my therapist taught me a few times and I finally feel like I'm getting some oxygen again.

Kade slides behind the bar and squats down, joining us. "That was him wasn't it?"

Kiersten nods but keeps her eyes on me. "Yep. Can you please call Paul? Tell him it's an emergency. He can just bring Carson and we'll figure that part out when they get here."

I grab my sister's hand and squeeze tightly, hoping her touch will anchor me to myself. I feel like I'm floating or having some sort of out of body experience. This can't be real. But it is.

"Kiersten." My words come out slow and quiet. "What do I do?"

She cups my cheek in her hand, making eye contact with me. It helps more than I expect it to—just to know she's right here with me. "Nothing. You wait until Paul gets here, okay? We'll figure this out. Just breathe."

Tucker's head pops over the counter. His eyebrows shoot up as he takes in the scene. I'm sure we look like a mess back here—me sitting on the floor trying not to pass out and Kiersten squatting next to me keeping me grounded.

For whatever reason, I suddenly decide I need to wait on my customer. It's like my brain is trying to find any bit of normal it can, so it goes on autopilot. As I try to stand, though, Kiersten pushes me back down to the floor.

"No. Stay sitting."

"But Tucker needs something," I argue flatly, unsure why it suddenly seems important to get back to work. "I need to… to… um, drink or something."

"They'll be fine without drinks for a bit, okay?"

I nod, still not completely sure I'm grasping the reality of the situation, but my legs are too wobbly to stand anyway.

Jeremy is back.

He came for me.

He's never going to leave me alone.

"Are you guys okay?" Tucker asks, concern written all over his face. "Who was that?"

"That," Kiersten says, her tone full of venom, "was her ex-boyfriend. The one who used to beat her. If you happen to see him walk into the bar again, feel free to kick him out. Or punch him out. Whatever."

I know that making him leave won't work though. I know it deep down.

Jeremy is back. He's never going to leave me alone. And I have no idea how I'm ever going to be okay again.

EIGHT

Kade

I'm working triple-duty now but the customers don't seem to mind. They may not have understood what exactly was happening, but they knew just by looking at Nicole and Kiersten that something bad was going down. It completely changed the laid-back vibe we had going.

Several people left shortly after the asshole ex did. The rest are uncharacteristically quiet and not giving me any shit for how long it's taking me to do the job of three people. Even Dwayne put away the pool cue for the night and is quietly chatting with another regular.

I, on the other hand, am still trying to calm down. When I saw that asshole's face, I wanted to punch him for every time he laid a hand on Nicole. I didn't. That's just not me. But if I was a bigger man, I would have beat him to a pulp and called it justice for her. Even now, I'm still seeing red. It makes it hard to concentrate on mixing drinks. Thank God almost everyone here is a beer drinker.

The door opens and I'm unsurprised when Heath and Jaxon walk in. They make a beeline straight for me. Heath doesn't even say hello before the questions start.

"What happened?"

"Her mom and ex-boyfriend showed up."

"Together?"

"Yep."

"Holy shit." Heath rubs his hand down his face. He's pissed. The anger is written all over him.

"It was rough," I continue giving more detail than is probably necessary but I need to get some of this out before I explode. "I'm surprised she stayed upright as long as she did. I've never seen that look on her face before. She was terrified."

"What happens now?" Jaxon slides onto the stool. Heath, on the other hand, is still pacing.

"I don't know. Paul is here and they've been holed up in the office ever since."

"I'll be right back." Heath heads to the back, presumably to find out what he can do to help. He's good like that.

Jaxon on the other hand stays put, drumming his fingers on the bar.

Sliding out from behind the counter, I grab the tray full of booze. "I'll be right back to get your drink."

He raises a hand. "Don't worry about me. I'm just here for moral support."

The first stop I make is to Tucker Hayes to deliver his IPA. Tucker is a relative newcomer but he's a nice guy, good tipper, maybe a little too flirty with Nicole but it goes with the job. As soon as I set it down in front of him, he stops whatever conversation he's having with his teammates and turns to me.

"I don't know what all happened, but when you see Nicole, let her know I have a bunch of guys at my disposal who would love nothing more than to track this guy down and show him what it feels like to be beaten on by someone bigger than you."

I almost want to laugh at how ridiculous he sounds, but to be honest, I want to give him the greenlight myself. I also want to know why he's so worried. He's new. He wasn't here when it happened. So why does it seem like he has a vested interest in making this right for Nicole?

I don't really want to know the answer to that and I'm a little bit exhausted from the last conflict to have any more today. "Sounds good, man. I'll let her know."

He gives me one solid nod and turns back to his friends.

Making my way around the room, I continue to field multiple questions about how Nicole is doing and what can be done to help her out, although none have quite the same violent solution as Tucker does. I give the same answer I've been using since the first time I made rounds without Nicole and Kiersten here—*"She's hanging in there. We'll let you know if there's anything you can do."* I don't know how true my answer is but I don't know what else to say either. I assume *"She's terrified so if you can bring his head back on a platter, that would be helpful"* is not the way to go. Besides, seems like Tucker has that covered anyway.

Once everything is delivered and everyone seems satisfied with their drinks, I go right back to work at the bar.

"Sorry about that." I store the tray out of the way but close enough to still load it up as I need to. Hopefully, I have a few minutes to talk to Jaxon. "Do you know what you want?"

"Just a longneck is good."

The request is easy enough and I'm thankful it gives me a bit of a reprieve from the pace I've been keeping for the last hour or so.

I place the drink in front of Jax and he immediately

takes a long swig, then puts it down and asks the question I wasn't expecting. "How are you holding up?"

"Me?" I furrow my brow in confusion. "I'm fine. It wasn't my ex-boyfriend."

"That's not what I mean. You just watched the girl you love have the worst shock of her life."

I scoff and grab a clean towel to begin wiping off the bar, but Jaxon keeps talking.

"Before you deny anything, I've been there. You don't know how Annika and I met but it was literally the worst night of her life. I'm not even exaggerating a little bit. It sucked and was gut-wrenching being there and watching how hard she worked to heal. So, I'm asking again, how are you holding up?"

I stop wiping and take a deep breath. "I'm angry," I say quietly.

"Understandable."

"He's big, man."

Jaxon glances up from his beer. "Bigger than Heath?"

That makes me smirk. "No one is bigger than Heath."

"Then this asshole isn't big enough to get through the entire Steer football team is he?"

I shake my head, hoping Jaxon is saying what I think he's saying. "No way."

"That's good. Because I have a feeling there's about to be some rotating patrons who spend their off nights here, drinking water."

"That'll really help, but what about when the bar is closed?" I sigh deeply, thinking about the shit show this is and the logistics of making sure Nicole is protected all the time. It's not my responsibility but that doesn't mean I don't want to be part of the solution. "She still lives here, which means he knows where her apartment is. I know

Paul has that place locked up with all kinds of security, but it still makes me nervous."

"Well, what can you do about it?" he asks, as if I haven't been wondering that same thing all night.

"I don't know. I want to move in or…or take her home with me so I know she's safe and he doesn't know where she is." I can hear the frantic hysteria in my voice. This is why I didn't want to talk about it and how I'm feeling. I'm feeling too much and I'm not sure what to do with it. I get back to wiping, my hands moving at a frantic pace.

"So why don't you?"

"Don't I what?"

"Take her home with you." He says it slowly like I'm missing the very obvious point. But I think he's missing the fact that we don't know each other that well.

"What? She wouldn't go for that."

"Why wouldn't she?"

I toss the towel on the counter and cross my arms. "Because I'm not an athlete and would have gotten pummeled if he'd thrown a punch tonight."

"Wait." Jaxon rears back. "Did you get in between them?"

He says it like it's some big gesture. As if he wouldn't have done the same thing. "She looked really scared. He didn't need to be looking at her and making her nervous. I just got in his line of sight."

A low whistle sounds from between his teeth. I narrow my eyes, not sure what conclusion he's come to.

"What?"

Pointing at me, he huffs a laugh. "You, my friend, have it bad. Even worse than I thought."

I roll my eyes and grab the towel again. "And here we go."

"Nope. Not again. This is new." He slides off the stool. "I'll be right back."

Confused, I watch as Jaxon walks right to the office and goes in without knocking.

"What the fuck is going on around here?" I mutter to myself but take the reprieve to check on all the tables again. When I'm confident everyone is still happy, I go back to my hiding spot behind the bar and keep busy with menial tasks. Just in time for Jaxon to return with Heath in tow.

Jaxon gestures to me. "Come to the back office."

"Um, I can't leave the bar unattended."

"Don't worry about that," he reassures, or tries to anyway. "Just come on."

"This is my job Jaxon," I say firmly. "I can't just leave. I'm the only one still here."

Heath cuts off our conversation when he puts his lips between his teeth and lets out a shrill whistle. The entire bar goes quiet.

"Hey, y'all. We have an urgent bar issue happening right now so I'm going to take over pouring drinks for a while. I've got…" he turns to look on the shelf behind me, "whiskey and whatever the hell is on tap. Those are your choices and you have to come ask for it because I'm not waiting on your sorry asses until this issue is resolved. Can you guys deal with that?"

There's a low rumble from the crowd, most everyone shrugging their shoulders and getting back to their conversations.

"Problem solved," Jaxon says. "Now come with me."

Heath and I trade places and I follow Jaxon into the back office, not sure if I'm about to get fired for that random changing of the guard, but I go with it. Call it curiosity and a strong need to make sure Nicole isn't still panicking.

The room feels tense, probably because Paul is pacing and looks like he wants to punch something. Kiersten is obviously still pissed. And Nicole is sitting on the couch, eyes blank like she's still in shock, rocking her nephew who is sound asleep on her lap. But her breathing is steady now, so that's good news.

When Paul finally notices me, his steps stop. "What's up. Everything okay out there?"

"Yeah," I answer, knowing he really doesn't care. His mind is on other more important things. "It's fine."

Jaxon immediately cuts in and gets to the point. "Kade has an idea and I think it's worth hearing him out."

I turn to look at him because, I do?

Oh right, I do.

I clench my hands into fists a couple of times to quell my nerves. One look at Nicole's face, though, and the anger surges again and I want to help this beautiful woman however I can.

"I was just thinking about how you live here. At the bar. And now that shithead knows where to find you. I don't like the idea of you being alone so I'm offering up the spare bedroom at my place. My roommate hasn't moved in yet, something about living with his girlfriend for a while, I don't know, I wasn't paying that much attention. But anyway, the room is free if you need it and it already has a bed and stuff."

Realizing I'm rambling, I stop abruptly.

Nicole gives me a small smile and I know Jaxon was right. This is the right thing to do. A way that I can protect her without getting either of us hurt in the process. I like this idea a lot better than trying to beat up anyone.

Paul turns tail and walks over to Nicole. "He's right. You can't stay here. You need to move in with us."

I deflate a little. I know I'm not family but it took a lot of courage for me to offer her a place to stay. I should know better than to get my hopes up.

"I'm not moving in with you Paul," Nicole says quietly as she strokes Carson's hair. "The offer is appreciated but we've had this conversation a hundred times and my answer hasn't changed."

"The hell it hasn't," Paul roars and Kiersten immediately shushes him. "That douchebag criminal wasn't in town before."

"I know. But I can't let that douchebag criminal re-arrange my life. I don't want to let him control me anymore. I'm staying here. Kade," she says turning back to me. "That was so nice of you. Like, the nicest thing anyone has ever done for me."

Pride fills my chest at her words. My offer may not have had the outcome I preferred, but I at least like her knowing she can come to me if she needs to.

"Ahem," Paul interjects making Nicole roll her eyes.

"The nicest thing by someone who isn't family or an overbearing alpha half the time."

I'm not sure if being alpha is a good or bad thing right now. From the look on Paul's face, I'm not sure if he does either.

"Truly," she continues, staring right at me. "I'll be okay."

"I just don't want you to be afraid," I admit in this room full of people who I'd rather not know my true feelings, but there it is.

"I don't either." Nicole shifts her nephew a bit and re-settles. "But I have to do this. I can't let him manipulate me, or any of us, just by walking in here. That's what he wants."

"Fuck," Paul mutters with a huff. He's obviously unhappy that Nicole would rather stay and fight than run and hide. I don't like it much either, but I get it. I understand that she doesn't want to take back all the progress she's made and I respect that.

"Okay," I finally say. "I get it. But just know, the offer is still open if you change your mind."

The smile she gives me is the first one I've seen since the ex-douche showed up. It gives me hope that she really is going to be okay and that's all I can really ask for.

"You'll be the first to know."

"Really?" Paul complains loudly.

"After Paul," she corrects with an amused grin that almost forces me to smile right back at her.

"Okay, well I'm gonna head back out there then." I gesture over my shoulder at the door. "Never know what's happening with Heath in charge."

"Jesus Christ," Paul grumbles. "What the hell is happening around here."

I suppress my chuckle as I get back to work. I'm still worried, but I feel better now. This is going to be difficult to power through, but at least Nicole seems up to the challenge. Even if Paul isn't.

NINE
Nicole

"Is that good enough Paul?" I yell through the door. "Did you hear the locks click and the alarm go on?"

"I didn't hear the chain yet," he yells back.

"Well, it's on."

"I didn't hear it. Do it again."

I sigh and roll my eyes but comply for his peace of mind. It's the least I can do considering how upset he is. I love that about him. He really is like the big brother I never had, all the way down to how overbearing he can be.

"I heard it that time," he hollers again. "You sure you're staying here?"

"I'm positive. Now go home with your family and get some rest."

"Okay. But keep your phone handy. And call me if you need anything. And call 911 if he comes back even though he won't if he knows what's good for him. And—"

"Good night, Paul!" I shout, cutting off his rant.

There's a short pause before I finally hear, "Yeah okay.

Good night."

I listen as his muffled footsteps fade away and finally, I feel like I can relax. There is no one staring at me or asking how I am or trying to make decisions on how I should feel. I'm well and truly…

Alone.

A small wave of panic runs through me as I realize there is safety in numbers, and right now there are no numbers. Only me. By myself. Maybe this wasn't such a good idea.

No.

No.

That's what he wants. He wants me to hide in fear. I won't give him that. I won't backpedal. I will stay strong.

I will also watch some television to stay distracted. There's always some mindless comedy on. I can focus on that. I'll be fine.

Grabbing the remote off the table I turn on the boob tube and search through the list of potential options until I find what I'm looking for. I already watched *The Circle*, but there's a French version I can try. That should do the trick.

Except… it doesn't. Even thirty minutes into it and some serious catfighting through the Circle Messenger, my mind is racing with thoughts. Wondering why mom would bring him here. Wondering why she doesn't believe me. Wondering if she gave up and went home.

I hate her role in all this. I hate that she's chosen a side and it's the wrong one. But she's my *mom*. I don't know that I can forgive her but I'm not sure how to let her go either.

Giving up on TV, I head toward the bathroom to start getting ready for bed and freeze…

My heart is pounding and it takes all my willpower to keep breathing normally. It's so dark in there. Too dark. I can't go in there.

Logically, I know there is nothing to be frightened of, but I still can't stop the fear that he's hiding in the shadows. I know, *know* he's not, but I can't get the panic under control. Come to think of it, the light in the bedroom area isn't on either.

I'm standing in the dark in the middle of the room.

I have no defense.

My feet begin to move before my brain catches up to what's happening. Soon I'm backed up against the wall, sliding over until I'm in a corner. I can see the entire room from this vantage point, even while sitting. Still, I have no weapon.

Looking around I see an old forgotten baseball bat under the couch. It has to be Paul's from when he lived here. He must have forgotten it when he moved in with my sister. Or, knowing him, he probably put it there on purpose so I'd have a weapon. I'm grateful for his overbearing ways as I quickly grab it and sit back in my hiding spot, bat in one hand and cell phone open and ready to call 911 in the other.

• • •

"You're mine, do you hear me?" His face is right in mine, his breath hot on my face. My arms ache from how hard his fingers are digging into my skin and I can't get away.

"Say it!" he roars. "Say you're mine!"

"I'm yours!" I yell frantically, praying he'll let me go.

His eyes turn darker, the white of his eyes all but disappearing. He doesn't just look evil. He looks like evil incarnate.

Pulling me closer, he makes sure our noses touch "No matter where you run, no matter how far away you get, I will always find you. No one can save you."

He pushes me away and I fly across the room, slamming into a wall and... I startle awake.

Breathing rapidly, I immediately pick up the bat that has rolled a couple of feet away from me and pull it up over my shoulder, ready to swing.

My eyes search the room for any sign of Jeremy, but he's not here.

I sink back into the wall and breath in, two, three, four… hold, two, three, four… and out, two, three, four… hold, two three, four.

It was only a nightmare.

I dig the heels of my hands into my eye sockets and feel myself waking up more. I must have dozed off at some point. The last time I looked at the clock it was six? Seven am? It's probably close to noon now. I can hear Kiersten's dance class beginning down the hall.

I feel terrible. My head is hurting and my body is aching. I'm sure it's a mixture of very little sleep and all of it on the floor. But now that there is some light shining in on the dark corners of the whole apartment, I feel a little better. Or at least I'm not as afraid.

Desperately needing to empty my bladder, I stumble to the bathroom, which thankfully has another small window above the shower so it's pretty bright in here. I go through the regular chores of washing my face and brushing my teeth. Then, making sure all the lights are on in the apartment, I collapse onto the bed and pray for a couple of hours of rest.

• • •

"You thought you could just move and get away from me?" He bellows, his fist suddenly in my stomach knocking the wind out of me.

"I own you. Own you!" And another fist, this one in my face. I hear and feel the cracks of my nose and blood sprays across the room.

"You bitch! Look what you made me do!" He's back in my face, screaming at me. "This wouldn't happen if you weren't such a whore!"

I rear back as his fist comes toward me again and... I startle awake again, tears streaming down my face.

He's got me. He did it. No matter how determined I am to not live in fear, there's no way to keep him out of my dreams.

I allow myself to cry for what seems like hours. Once the tears finally dry up, I peel myself up from the bed and wash my face again. There is no way makeup is going to hide the brutality of this night. I have deep, dark circles and my whole face is puffy. I'll just have to hope we're busy tonight and no one has time to take a good look at my face.

Wandering back into the small living room area, I grab my phone. I have two missed calls and three missed texts. Almost all of them are from my sister.

Even worse, it's only two in the afternoon. I didn't even get a full night's sleep and what little rest I did get, I was fighting off Jeremy in my dreams. This sucks.

Plopping down on the couch, I curl my feet underneath me and call Kiersten back. It only rings once before she picks up.

"Hello?" she sounds frantic. "Nicole, are you okay?"

No. No, I'm not. I'm terrified of being alone at night and my nightmares are plaguing me no matter what time

I sleep.

"I'm fine," I lie. I hate not telling her the truth, but if I do, it'll turn into a bigger thing than it needs to be otherwise.

"Are you sure?" She doesn't sound convinced.

"I'm sure. How was your class, anyway? Sounded like you were having fun. I could hear you down here."

"It was fine. Don't change the subject," she demands. "Did you sleep at all?"

No. "Yes."

"Did you sleep well?"

"Do I ever sleep well?"

"Not my point but okay. I'll drop it. Are you sure you're okay? Tammy and Kade are working tonight. I'm trying to keep Paul from coming in to check on you but I'm having a hard time convincing him."

I groan, my head dropping on the headrest behind me. "Tell him if he comes in, I quit and I'm moving out."

That finally elicits a small laugh from her. "Will do. But really, if you need anything you promise you'll call?"

"Kiersten, you will always be the first person I call if I need something."

"Don't let Paul hear you say that." Now it's my turn to laugh. He's so good to us, but he's also so fun to poke at. "I'll let you go then. Good luck tonight. I love you."

"I love you too. Give Carson the biggest hug from me."

We hang up and I spend some time on my couch, trying to get into the French version of *The Circle* but still to no avail. I finally give up and start getting ready for work. I know I'll probably flinch every time the door opens tonight, but it could be worse. Staying here last night is proof of that. I'll figure something out, though. I always do.

TEN
Kade

Somehow, I'm managing the bar tonight. It was already on the schedule so that part isn't a surprise. I just figured Paul would be taking over after last night's surprise visitor. I'm sure he's dying to be here. Unfortunately for him, Carson has some sort of school program tonight that neither he nor Kiersten can miss so they're both off.

I kind of feel bad for Kiersten. She's the one who has to stop Paul from showing up here anyway. The thought gives me the slightest bit of amusement. *Overbearing Paul* is kind of funny.

My biggest concern is I don't want any more unwanted guests here tonight. I don't like the idea of having to call the cops any more than I want to see Nicole collapse again. The look she had when that fucker was here haunted me all night long. I've never seen anyone that afraid, except in horror movies. I knew that's what she was feeling—horror. I never want to see it again if I can help it.

The only thing I'm looking forward to is Tammy waitressing. She's entertaining enough to keep our minds off heavier topics. Case in point, for whatever reason, tonight she's decided to learn all about gaming. I have no idea why, but unsurprisingly, she has very strong opinions.

"I will never understand these video games you kids like so much." She grabs an apron off the shelf and begins tying it around her waist while she rants. "What is fun about hunting a fake duck? That won't feed you dinner."

I laugh to myself, knowing I have never played *Duck Hunter* before. She'd probably fall over if she ever found out what *Call of Duty* is about. Still, it gives me the opportunity to chide her a bit and I could use the laugh. "You're telling me you don't cook the ducks your husband hunts in real life?"

She rears back and grimaces. "Hell no. Those poor things are riddled with disease."

I have no response except to shake my head as she goes off to continue setting up for the night. She'll undoubtedly be back with more opinions later.

I hear the apartment door close down the hall and look up to see Nicole practically dragging her way out here. She looks exhausted. Still beautiful, but also like she stayed up all night.

Her hair, which is normally down around her shoulders, is tied up high in one of those messy bun things. She has makeup on, but it's clear she's trying to hide deep, dark circles under her eyes. She's even wearing glasses, which I never knew she needed. I want to take her in my arms, turn us right back around, and go tuck her into bed with a kiss on the forehead. That's not my place though. I greet her normally instead.

"Hey. Nice glasses."

Her cheeks pinken just a bit. "Thanks."

"No contacts today?"

One shoulder raises in a small shrug. "I don't really need the glasses very much. It's not like I'm totally blind without them. But labels will be hard to read otherwise and I'd rather not have to do twice the work because I keep screwing up drink orders."

"Smart idea." I grab a stack of bowls to being filling with snacks. "How are you feeling anyway?"

"I wish people would quit asking me that."

I fumble with the bowl I'm using to scoop pretzels as a wave of embarrassment hits me. "I'm sorry. I'm not trying to pry into your personal life."

She sighs deeply and her shoulders drop in resignation. "No. Please don't be sorry. I'm the one who should apologize. It was a rough night. You were there. You know."

I suspect there's more to that statement than she's telling me, but I let it go. "Nicole, there's no reason to apologize. You've had a lot of people hovering over you for the last, well, eighteen plus hours."

She pauses our conversation briefly to clock in and slide behind the counter. "Everyone means well. It was just a long night and I shouldn't take it out on you. You've been so sweet to me for months and I really like being around you. You make me feel calm."

Me?

"I do?"

Her lips quirk up and she nods. "I see the way you scoop up the crickets that get in the building and toss them outside so they can finish out their lives in the grass, instead of stomping the guts right out of them. I think you've got a good heart."

I've only done that once and I didn't know anyone caught me in the act. That makes me feel good. But I also notice she didn't say I was a good protector or an alpha male. I know I'm not either of those things but I wish she thought I was.

"Anyway," she says with another sigh as she pulls out the fruit to slice. "My sister and Paul are just getting on my nerves. I feel bad about it. They've done so much for me. Sometimes I think they have a little bit too much interest in my life, though."

"Be glad you have that. I don't have many people who are interested in my life at all."

I didn't mean to say that out loud but now that we've gotten over our awkward conversation stage, I find myself saying things I later regret.

Nicole gasps, her eyes wide in question. "But why not? You're such a great person."

She seems truly shocked but it's not a painful thing to me. It's my normal. "I'm a video game nerd and I'm not good-looking like Jaxon or athletic like Heath. I never really had any friends in high school and college is better, but still has a lot of cliques. I just don't fit in anywhere."

"What about your family?"

This is more than I ever wanted to share with her about what a loser I am, but if it makes her feel better about all the support she has, I'll suck it up and tell her. "Let's just say my mother loves partying more than she loves being a parent. And I don't know who my dad is so I kind of grew up alone."

"Wait." I know what's coming. This is the part people always get stuck on. "I thought you and Jaxon had the same dad."

"We thought so for a while but the DNA proved us wrong. Jaxon just never told anyone the results when we found out. Doesn't matter anyway. His dad died a couple of months before I was born so it's not like I would have had the chance to meet him."

"Well, it's all their loss," Nicole says with conviction. "I think you're an amazing human being and less time with them just means more time with me."

God, she's beautiful. And so nice and sweet. I think I would fall over and die if she ever agreed to go on a date with me. Not that I'm going to ask. A girl like her can do so much better than a guy like me.

I clear my throat and hope my face isn't flaming red right now. It's doubtful. I can feel the heat radiating from my cheeks at her compliment.

"Thank you for that. Can you handle getting the bowls ready, too? I need to grab the money out of the safe."

"Sure. No problem."

I leave as quickly as I can, not because the money can't wait. It can. The till isn't usually filled until the last minute anyway. I just don't know how much longer I can stay physically away from her. I need a second to regroup and breathe where I can't smell the scent she uses. She's the only person I know who wears it and it may very well bring me to my knees.

Dropping down on the couch, I give myself a few extra minutes to get my bearings straight before getting what I need from the safe and heading back out to the front. It's a good thing, too. Tucker Hayes is already hitting on Nicole. I try hard to not let it sour my mood and to maintain some form of friendliness.

"Hey man." I slide behind the counter and open the register to begin sorting the cash. "What's going on?"

It's weird that Tucker is here sitting at the bar before we're open, and I'm not sure why Nicole let him in early, but I have a feeling he's not here for a beer.

"I'm sorry for intruding like this, man. I know you're

not open yet. I just wanted to get here before anyone else showed up and ask if you need help tonight."

I furrow my brow. What does he mean by help?

"Like, with security and stuff," he says answering my unasked question.

That's when it hits me. Tucker is here to make sure Nicole feels safe while she's at work. It's a blow to my ego to know yet another person doesn't think I can protect her.

On the other hand, I probably can't. Setting my pride aside for a few seconds, I realize he probably is more evenly matched against that Jeremy guy if it came down to it. I hate it, but I care for Nicole more than I hate my own flaws.

Nicole puts her hand on his forearm and I don't think I've ever been more jealous in my life. "You don't have to do that Tucker. It's really nice of you, but I'll be fine. Besides, I'm sure you have an early morning practice."

"No, wait," I blurt out. I hate that I agree with him, especially since I see the way he looks at her, but I'd feel better if we had someone like him as an extra set of eyes. I'll think about how much it hurts that he's the kind of guy she deserves later. "Are you serious, man?"

"Sure," he says with a shrug of indifference, but I know he's anything but. I can see it in the way his eyes keep darting around the room. "I thought about it all night. I know there's not a lot any of us can do, but maybe just sitting here will be enough, ya know? Like a show of support from some guys who could do some damage to his face. Or better yet, his balls."

"Come on, guys. This is all unnecessary," Nicole argues, smiling like always but it looks forced. Almost like she's trying to convince herself more than us.

"I have to agree with Tucker on this one," I say as I

close and secure the register. "If we get busy, we won't even see him walk in. I'd rather have someone sitting at this bar who is specifically here for that reason."

"What reason? What's going on with all this jibber-jabbering?" Tammy interrupts, probably expecting some juicy gossip. But I don't know if she's even aware of everything that happened last night yet. We'll have to tell her soon, but her attentions are on Tucker right now. "And what are you doing here so early, pretty boy? Got lady problems and couldn't wait for a few extra minutes?"

Nicole makes eye contact and I know she's wondering the same thing I am. Did Paul call Tammy or did he leave this up to us to take care of?

Tucker clasps his hands together and fidgets with his cuticles. It's obvious he isn't sure how to answer Tammy. He probably doesn't want her to know he's here because he's been thinking about Nicole all night. Hell, I don't even want to know that. It kind of makes me want to kick his ass to the curb.

"I'm good. Just here to hang with Nicole if she needs me."

Tammy winks at me. I'm pretty sure she's trying to be conspiratorial but she's failing miserably. Still, we've got bigger problems to worry about right now and since I'm the manager on duty, I guess it falls to me to address.

"Tammy, did Paul happen to call you and let you know about what happened last night?"

She diverts her attention over to me. "You mean about Nicole's ex-ass showing up? Sure did."

"Why didn't you say anything?" Nicole sounds as confused as I am. Tammy loves a good, juicy story. I assumed she would have jumped all over this one.

She surprises us all when she says, "I figured you

already had enough people hovering over you, honey. Thought you might like at least one person in your life to act normal and not tiptoe around you."

Nicole's face softens. "How did you know I needed that?"

"I have lived a lot of life, honey. More than any of you youngins know about. It's made me wise in my years." Turning back to Tucker she finally puts it all together. "Is that why you're here? You gonna be her personal bouncer all night?"

"That was the plan." Tucker looks back up at Nicole, and I see the overwhelming *like* in his stupid pretty eyes. "If she'll let me."

"It's not about letting you. You have practice in the morning don't you?"

"Not an early one," he admits. "Besides, it's not like I'm pulling an all-night bender and then going in. I've done that before." He shakes his head and blows out a breath. "That morning was brutal. If I can get through that, I can easily do this."

Tammy waves off Nicole's concern. "See honey? It might be a little out of everyone's way. But it'll make the men around here feel like they're doing somethin' important and if I've learned anything over close to thirty years of marriage, it's that men like to feel needed." I suppose she's not wrong about that, even if it is an outdated stereotype. "And besides," she leans in, lowering her voice to speak like we can't hear her as the only people in this very small area. "It just gives me a little bit of eye candy for the evening and you wouldn't want to deny an old woman of that, would you?"

Nicole puts her fingers over her lips and tries not to giggle. "Oh, well, in that case, I guess he has to stay then, doesn't he?"

Tammy smacks the counter with her hand once. "Then it's settled. Non-alcoholic drinks on the house for tonight's bouncer. What tickles your fancy tonight, hockey boy? A soft drink or maybe a virgin daiquiri?"

"I'll just stick with a bottled water if you have it."

"Coming right up. Kade!" she hollers even though I'm right here. "I've got an order of bottled water for the eye candy at the bar."

I just shake my head as I grab the water and place it in front of him. Like I said, if nothing else, at least Tammy will keep us all entertained.

ELEVEN
Nicole

I recognize most of the irritation I feel, and display, is misplaced nerves.

I don't know how I would have made it through the past year without Paul playing the role of overprotective big brother and my sister playing, well, my overprotective big sister. I'm so grateful for them. But I'm also grateful for the people here at my work.

Who knew that everyone would jump into action the second there was even a minor threat of trouble? I've never experienced anything like it before. It makes me wonder where everyone was the two years I was dating Jeremy. Did no one notice or did they just not care that I had random bruises I explained away as accidents? Regardless, it just confirms that I made the right decision leaving everything behind to move here. What it doesn't do, however, is ease my anxiety.

As the night goes on, I get more and more nervous. Every time the door opens, I jump and have a flood of fear run through me, praying it's not *him* again. Even worse,

I don't want to go back into that apartment. I'm surviving this night on caffeine and the absolute desire to not go home, but time is running out before everyone leaves, and I'm not sure what to do.

The last patron finally heads out the door and Tammy turns the locks behind him. Even Tucker is already gone now that the evening is over.

"What a night." She stretches out her arms to relieve the muscles in her back. "I love having those boys hang out but, whoo-wee. They are some high maintenance drama queens, aren't they?"

Kade chuckles in response. I would, too but I'm busy fretting about what I'm going to do when they leave. How am I going to make it through the night again?

I don't know if I'm wiping the counter a little too hard or if I have a strange look on my face or if I've been snippy all night, but suddenly Kade is next to me.

"Are you okay?"

"SureYeahWhy?" My answer comes out way too quickly and I know I've blown any cover I had.

"You just look like you want to throw up."

"That's not a flattering thing to say to a girl," I try to joke in a bad attempt at playing off my real feelings. It falls flat though and he doesn't take the bait.

"Are you afraid to go to your apartment alone?"

My movements stop. Closing my eyes, I drop my chin to my chest. "I'm really that transparent?"

"If I wasn't here last night, I might not have put it together, but I was. And I'm not stupid. Nicole," he puts his hand on my arm, stopping my circular motions that have started again on the bar top. It's the first time he's closed that two-foot gap between us, and I'm grateful for the contact. "The offer to come home with me is still good." His eyes widen and he holds his hands up defensively. "Not like that. I don't mean it like that. I mean so you're not by yourself. And you're not with Paul either."

I can't help but smirk at his nervousness. "Kade, I can't inconvenience you like that."

"It's not an inconvenience," he continues to argue and I can feel myself beginning to cave. "Really. It's one friend helping another friend out during a time of need. I'm just providing a service."

I tilt my head at him, trying not to laugh. His face begins to turn red like it always does when he's embarrassed or nervous.

"Not a service," he tries for the backpedal. "That sounded shady or like I'm an escort. Clearly, I'm not an escort. I don't have the abs for it. Okay, I'm going to stop now."

"Your offer is so sweet," I say with a smile. "I just," I sigh again feeling overwhelmed. I feel like all I do these days is inconvenience everyone. "It feels like running away. I don't want him to drive me out of my own apartment and give him more control, you know?"

"I do. I totally know. But I also know you'll have a harder time combatting this if you don't get enough sleep. And you didn't get any last night, did you?"

I shake my head. "That obvious, huh? Was it the glasses or the hairstyle that clued you in?"

"Neither. I watch you all the time when no one is looking so I know every detail of your face, which means I can tell. I also just said too much again, didn't I?" He squeezes the bridge of his nose and grumbles, "Oh boy. This night isn't ending well for me."

I bite back a grin. Maybe my feelings aren't as unrequited as I thought. "I like that you enjoy my face so much."

"I do. Enjoy it. So please say you'll just spend one night so you can rest."

"Take the boy up on his offer," Tammy interjects loudly as she slides behind the counter and places more dirty glasses in the sink. "You don't have to sleep with him but at least mess around a little bit and get in out of your systems."

"Tammy!" I admonish, but that woman has no shame.

"What? When did everyone turn into such prudes around here?" She heads back out front, a clean dishrag in her hands.

Kade follows her with his eyes, shaking his head. "The good news is I can always count on Tammy to make things even more awkward between us."

I giggle at Kade's retort. "I'm pretty sure that's why she does it. And she calls the guy's drama queens."

"Well, I can promise there won't be any making out tonight, but I really think you should at least spend one night in my guest room. You don't have to stay any longer than you want, but at least it'll give you a night to think through things and decide if you want to stay longer."

He makes a good point. Just one night of decent sleep will probably make a world of difference.

"Okay," I finally agree. "But just one night."

He holds up his hands and backs away slowly. "I would never pressure you for more." Turning on his heel, he gets back to work balancing the till.

With three of us here, it doesn't take long to close up shop. Once tips are divvied out and everything is shut down, Tammy leaves.

Kade, on the other hand, follows me to my apartment so I can quickly pack a bag. I'm grateful he comes with me. Out of habit, I left all the lights off so it's pitch-black when we walk in. I'm not sure I'd make it past the doorway if he wasn't with me.

I grab only the necessities—toiletries, jammies, clothes for a couple of days just in case, and feminine products because I'm so irregular, I never know what to expect—while Kade wanders around the small area.

"I didn't even realize this apartment was back here until a few months ago," he calls out as I toss my face products in a toiletry bag.

"You've only worked here for a few months."

"Right. But it took me a solid two of those to figure out you weren't going in and out of a storage room or office or something."

Coming around the corner, I stop to get the bags situated. "You didn't think it was weird that I never left at closing?"

"I honestly never thought about it. Maybe I assumed you slipped out when I wasn't looking or something."

"It's not big." I zip up my bag and stand up straight, stretching out my back a bit. "But the place fits me okay and the price was right."

"Price?"

"Free."

"Ah." Kade does a slow nod and looks around again. "You can't beat that deal. Are you ready?"

Grabbing my bag, I fling it over my shoulder. "Let's go."

Kade opens the door for me and waits while I lock up the apartment. And then I return the favor as he goes into manager-on-duty mode and finishes locking up the front.

We walk side by side in comfortable silence to his car. It's a beat-up old Chevy Tahoe, probably circa the early

1990's. It's definitely seen better days, but the inside is clean and I learn quickly that Kade likes to follow all traffic laws. It's three in the morning and he stops at every stop sign and looks both ways, even with absolutely no traffic on the roads.

His apartment is about five minutes away in an older neighborhood, but the building is in nice shape. It's clear whoever owns the apartment complex takes good care of the place.

Even the inside is nice. The countertops could use an upgrade but the cabinets look to be freshly painted in the kitchen and bathroom Kade shows me.

"Is this a furnished apartment?"

He looks at me curiously. "No."

"Oh." I place my bag down on the spare bed and continue to eye the room. "Since it already has a bed in here, I just assumed."

"Oh, no. It's my roommate's bed, actually. He asked me to store it for him and what else am I going to use this room for? It's been doubling as a guest room for the summer."

"Have you had a lot of guests?"

"You're actually the first one." He bites his bottom lip and shoves his hands in his pockets before remembering something and scurrying out of the room. "I'll be right back."

I take a few moments to look around the space again, appreciating that Kade would offer it up to me. He was right about coming here. The whole place feels homey and lived in, but in a good way. Like I can relax and just think. That's better than being in my place where all I can do is freak out. Hopefully, I'll even get a little sleep tonight.

Kade reenters the room and places a stack of linens on

the bed next to my bag.

"There's a big towel and a face towel and a washcloth. I wasn't sure which ones you would need so I brought them all. And I'm sorry the sheets don't match but they're worn in just enough to be comfortable. They're my favorites so I hope you like them." He clears his throat and I know he's nervous about me being here. I'm afraid he's afraid I won't be comfortable and I don't like that feeling.

"If they're you're favorite, then I'm sure they'll be perfect," I reassure him. And probably also me.

He nods once and his shoulders relax. "You should get some sleep."

I sink down onto the bed and shove my hands between my thighs. "It's going to take me a while to calm down enough to rest."

"Because you're still afraid or…?"

The concern on his face is so endearing, I don't have the heart to not correct him. "I'm still amped up from that part, sure. But mostly it's because we just got off work. It takes a while to wind down."

"You… wanna play *Red Dead Redemption* with me?" he asks while fidgeting with the band around his wrist.

"What?"

"*Red Dead Redemption*. It's a video game. It usually helps me unwind after work."

It hits me that he's offering me a way to deescalate and distract myself from whatever ugly thoughts I might have. I don't know how I missed that before. "Isn't that a war game or something?"

He snickers at my very basic description. Obviously, I'm not a gamer. "Not really. It's more like Gunsmoke on steroids, I guess. It's won a whole bunch of awards because of how much there is to do and all the storylines. You can play online or by yourself. It's fun."

I admit, I'm kind of stunned. "I had no idea there were video game awards and that it was so complex."

"Oh yeah. It's very intense. Been around for almost twenty years and they've got a second version, but I want to finish the first before I move on. You can play with people all over the world, too. We don't have to do that tonight, though. They're probably all asleep anyway."

I bite my bottom lip, oddly interested in seeing what this is all about. Or maybe I'm just intrigued because Kade is obviously passionate about it.

"Are you sure you want to teach me how to play? I'll probably get killed in the first thirty seconds and that would be really boring for you."

He looks down and shoves his hands in his pockets again. "I don't think it'll be boring. Not with you, it won't. Not at all."

I can't help the flutters in my stomach from his words. I don't know if he's interested in me or is just trying to be nice, but either way, he makes me feel good.

Hands on my thighs, I push up to standing again. "Do you mind if I shower the bar off me first? I feel really sticky."

"Sure. Yeah. Of course." Kade slowly backs up, clearly feeling awkward but I'm not sure why. "I should… yeah… I need to do that too so, take your time." His back hits the wall and he bounces off quickly, turning to the doorway and muttering, "Sorry," then turning back to me. "Um, yeah I'll be out there whenever you're ready."

And then he's gone, with me standing there baffled by what just happened, but not worried about it enough to keep me from a nice, hot shower and a few minutes to process all my thoughts.

TWELVE
Kade

"Shoot him! Shoot him!" I command like the drill sergeant I pretend I am but nothing happens.

"Why isn't this button working?" Nicole practically squeals, her controller moving around like it's a steering wheel because that's going to help her shoot.

"Because you need the other one! Press the other button! Get him!"

Before she can get the shot off, it's over. The wild boar came out of nowhere and gored her right on the spot.

Nicole drops her controller in her lap in defeat. "Oh, man. I was so close to getting on that train."

She really wasn't. But I don't bother telling her that. She's been smiling and laughing for two hours. I don't want to take the fun away from her. I opt to go the encouraging route instead.

"You're definitely getting better."

Her eyes light up like I just told her she won a million bucks. Who knew *Red Dead Redemption* could make her so happy. "Really?"

I fumble with my controller and refuse to make eye contact. She's not getting *that* much better. "You lasted a solid four and half minutes this time."

She huffs and throws herself back on the couch. "It took us three of those just to get on the horse and get into the wild West."

"And you didn't get shot off your horse. That's better than Archie, half the time."

She punches me playfully, a laugh bursting out of her. This is the most fun I've had for as long as I can remember. Nicole was terrible at the game, absolute shit, but she had so much fun. Next time I'll have to let her play when my normal friends are on. They like to give me shit about working with a girl of Nicole's caliber. I'd like to give them a taste of their own medicine and see what kind of awkward conversations they try to have with her.

It's not that all gamers are geeks who can't get girl-friends. It's just that my particular crowd is exactly like that. Archie lives in his mom's basement. He's alluded to having some sort of disability but it's not my business so I never ask for details. And Rodney is married and like thirty-seven or something. Totally weird that he prefers spending his nights online with us than his wife but again, not my business.

The only one of us I'd consider relatively normal is Matty of course. He's the one I'll need to keep an eye on should I decide to bring Nicole into the fold. I know him well enough to know he'd try hitting on her the whole time. I'll have to keep reminding everyone he's in high school and lives with his parents. That's about all I've got over him. Even standing next to him, he towers over me.

"You wanna go again?" I ask just as she covers her mouth to let out the biggest yawn I've ever seen. "Or maybe you need to get some sleep instead."

"Sorry," she says through her hand. "I didn't sleep much last night so I think I'm starting to crash."

"Yes. Of course." I feel so stupid for not remembering the whole reason she's staying here tonight. It's not about having a slumber party. It's about her finally getting some sleep.

Taking the controller from her hand, I make quick work of putting everything away. "Before you hit the hay, do you need anything? I gave you enough blankets, right?"

"It's barely October in San Antonio. I'm going to be just fine."

"Right." It seems I've thought of everything. Except how to exit this conversation and go to bed without sounding like a total dimwit.

She pushes up from the couch, moves close to me and I hold my breath as her lips get closer…

And closer…

And closer…

And suddenly my stomach is jumping as she's leaving a kiss on my cheek.

"Thank you for everything, Kade," she whispers in my ear and I swear I've lost all ability to speak, move, think, basically anything with her this close to me. "Good night."

She slowly pulls away, making sure to give me a shy smile before walking into the spare bedroom and closing the door behind her, leaving me as stiff as a statue.

Speaking of stiff, I suddenly need to take another shower. Well, as soon as I can get my brain and body to connect again.

Finally, I'm able to blow out a breath and move, although it's still feeling surreal that she kissed me. And yes, I know it was just on the cheek, but it had to mean something right? Or maybe it doesn't and I'm overthinking it.

Either way, I have to hop in the shower again, hoping she doesn't hear the water running. She'll for sure know what I'm up to. I'm pretty sure she knew it was going to happen before we even started playing.

As I rid myself of my pajama pants and shirt, I climb into the water jet, thinking about how she looked freshly showered and in her own nighttime clothes.

No makeup on her freshly washed face. Hair still damp from the shower. She was just wearing polka dot jammie pants and a hoodie, but it didn't matter that she wasn't wearing sexy lingerie. She still looked like my most daring fantasy. She looked intimate. Like it was part of her she was sharing only with me. Especially when her nipples poked through and I knew she wasn't wearing a bra.

I take my dick in my hand and begin giving it long, leisurely strokes. I wonder if this is what it would feel like to push inside of her. To feel her heat wrapped around me. To see her eyes widen ever so slightly, her mouth forming into an "o" as the tip of my dick found that sweet spot inside her, making her come.

My strokes become fast as I wonder, would she moan? Would she yell my name? Would she hold her breath as her eyes roll back into her head, bliss taking over as she scrapes her fingernails down my back? Would her body squeeze me as tightly as I'm squeezing myself right now, catapulting me into my own bliss?

It takes just a few more pumps before I find my release and my fantasy fades away. I don't think I've ever come that quickly, and certainly not from my imagination. Usually, I need to watch a bit of porn to have something to go on, but not with Nicole. Freshly showered Nicole playing video games is better than anything porn can do for me.

I spend a few minutes cleaning up and then I'm out of the shower again, ready to hit the hay. While I wouldn't trade it for anything, it's been a long night and I need some sleep if I'm going to make it to my eleven o'clock class.

As I pull on my basketball shorts and t-shirt, I hear something from down the hall. Pausing, I realize it's Nicole. And she's yelling.

My heart picks up speed as I race out my bedroom door and across the apartment, ready to call 911 to come arrest the asshole who's broken in and has ruined the calm she was finally feeling. Flinging open her bedroom door, I stop dead in my tracks.

There's no one else here. At least not in the apartment. Inside her dreams is another story.

The nightmare looks fierce, Nicole is thrashing around, tears running down her face as she sleeps. My heart breaks for her, that she can't get away from this man even in her sleep.

"Nicole," I call out in a loud whisper, afraid of startling her. "You're okay. It's just a dream." Not wanting to invade her space, I'm still standing in the doorway. Unfortunately, it doesn't work so I go inside a little further.

"No!" She yells, eyes still closed. "No!"

"Nicole. Wake up. You're having a nightmare," I say a little louder this time. She still doesn't respond.

I get next to the bed but make sure not to touch her, afraid she'll interpret my touch as a threat to her safety. "Nicole? You're okay. I need you to wake up now." I'm speaking at a normal volume now, desperate to wake her up.

She's still in the throes of her nightmare and I feel so helpless. The longer this goes on, the worse it's going to be for her. The deeper she'll get into feeling like it's reality. I make the decision to touch her, shake her arm, speak louder, and do everything I can to wake her quickly. "Nicole! Wake up. He's not here. He's not here!"

She startles and pulls away from me, but at least she stops thrashing and her eyes peel open. She's not quite coherent, but she's getting there.

Finally, she looks up, confused by what is reality and what is not. "Kade?"

I lower my volume again, not wanting to scare her. "He's not here. You're having a dream. Everything is okay."

She relaxes into the bed as it finally dawns on her what is going on. Her blue eyes look up at me and her brows furrow as tears roll down her face. Not sure what to do, I keep my hand on her arm, until she pulls me down to her and wraps her arms around me.

Instinctually, I climb onto the bed with her and wrap her in the blanket and my arms as she sobs. I know she needs to feel safe and it's the only thing I can do to help her.

"Shhh… it's okay," I whisper in her ear as she continues to cry. "I know it was scary but it's over. You got through it and you never have to do that again."

She stays wrapped up, me rubbing circles on her back until she finally falls asleep. I feel so conflicted. While I want to memorize the feeling of her body next to mine, more than anything I wish there was no reason for me to be holding her at all.

THIRTEEN
Nicole

I t's been two weeks since I moved in. Two weeks since that awful night. Two weeks since Kade held me all night long and made my nightmares go away.

He has never climbed in bed with me again.

Of course, I haven't asked him to because that would be way too forward of me, but part of me wishes he would offer. I know he doesn't like me like that, or at least, I'm not really sure and don't want to make him uncomfortable, but somehow, I felt really safe with him in bed with me. I don't understand why. It's not like either of us could fight off Jeremy if he broke in and went ballistic. And yet, Kade soothes me. He takes the edges off my terror. The fear is still there, but when Kade is around, he dims it to a manageable level.

It also helps that I haven't seen Jeremy again. It makes me nervous and my mind still spins with all my concerns as to what is happening, but the logical one is that is he gave up when he got a less than welcome reception. I don't remember a lot from the night my mom blindsided us, but in hindsight, I'm sure it was disconcerting to have an entire bar full of huge athletes go silent as they watched the events unfold. While I'm not totally convinced he's gone for good, he'd be smart to stay away.

Me, on the other hand, I'm tired of working or hanging around Kade's apartment. I could go back to mine, but I like being here. Kade is fun to have as a roommate and I'm getting pretty decent at *Red Dead Redemption*. Or at least I'm better. I made it a whole eight minutes the other day before falling off the roof of the bank.

I hear Kade's keys drop on the kitchen counter as he gets back from class.

"Nicole?" he calls out before poking his head around the corner. "Are you decent?"

I laugh at how ridiculous he looks with his hand over his eyes, just in case I'm in my unmentionables.

"You can put your hand down, weirdo. If I wasn't decent I'd be in the bedroom with the door closed."

Leaning against the doorframe of the small hall bathroom, he watches as I pull a section of my hair through my wave iron and press the plates closed.

"What are you doing to your hair?" He sounds thoroughly confused as to what he's seeing.

"I'm wave ironing it."

"Why?" His nose crinkles adorably like I'm doing physics and not hair care.

"To give myself that wind-tossed beach look."

"We don't live near a beach."

Amused, I release the plates and move down a notch to get the next section. "That's no excuse to not have great hair."

He looks around the small room, likely taking in everything I have in here. I don't think I fully knew how much I had until I slowly began bringing things over and setting them up on the small counter.

"It really takes all this stuff to give you those… waves, or whatever?"

Placing the wave iron on the counter, I section off another part of my hair and spray it with some heat protector. "It all has different purposes but short answer—yes. All this stuff is necessary if I want to look my best."

"Huh." He sounds completely baffled. "I use this three in one shampoo and body wash Jaxon gave me. I feel like I'm missing something."

I offer him a bemused smile in the reflection of the mirror. "I guess some of us just need more help than others."

"Not you. You're perfect."

My gaze whips up to his and his eyes widen slightly, as if he just realized he said that out loud.

Clearing his throat, he bites his bottom lip before quickly changing the subject. "Why are you getting dressed up anyway?"

"It's not really dressed up. I'm just going to run to the store and didn't want to end up on some derogatory webpage."

He chuckles and pushes off from the doorway. "Okay. Let me grab a sandwich real quick and I'll go with you."

Placing the wave iron on the counter I flip it to the "off" position and run my fingers through the waves. "You don't have to if you want to relax and take a load off."

Satisfied I haven't missed any spots on my hair, I grab my favorite gloss and twist it open. That's when I realize Kade hasn't responded to me. Glancing up, I see him worrying his lip again.

Trying for eye contact and failing, I say gently, "He hasn't been around at all, Kade. It might actually be time for me to go back to my apartment."

His shoulders slump. "Are you sure you really want to do that? I mean, like, you don't think you'll be scared or whatever?"

I don't really know the answer to that. I won't know until I try getting back to my life. "I'll be okay," I say reassuringly. "Besides, your roommate will be moving in any day now, right? I need to clear out so he can get in."

Kade lowers his head and grumbles. "Yeah, that asshole decided at the last minute he wasn't moving in."

"What! Oh no! You really do need a roommate as soon as possible."

"It could be you."

I blink rapidly several times, shocked by his suggestion. "You… you would want me to stay? Even with all my drama?"

"Of course. You're a great roommate. You're clean. You smell better than the last guy." I can't help my giggle at that. "And you're finally getting the hang of *Red Dead Redemption*. It would be a shame for you to lose all that practice time when you're so close to levelling up."

"That's really nice of you to consider me, Kade." And now that he's brought it up, I'm wondering if it might be a good idea. Yes, it'll cost me more in rent, but he's right, I like living here. It's quieter than living at the bar and means Paul has to give me a little more space. It's something for me to at least think about. "How soon do you need to know?"

He shrugs and I have a feeling he wouldn't care if I just never left, agreement or not. "Whenever. There's no rush."

"How about I let you know in a couple of days?"

He bites his lip again only this time he's trying to hold back the grin I see trying to come out. "That sounds perfect."

I take a deep breath and turn on my heel. "Well. I am headed to the store for some things you don't want to know about."

His brows furrow until suddenly the lightbulb goes off. "Lady products. Got it. Yeah, I'm not going."

"I swear guys are so weird. Do you need anything while I'm there?"

"Nope. No. Nada." He stumbles over his words, probably still fixed on the fact I need more tampons. Men are so weird. "Unless you need chocolate or ice cream or something. Wait. Do you need chocolate? Maybe you should sit down and I'll go."

I put my hand on his shoulder and force eye contact. "A period is not life-threatening, Kade. You can take a deep breath."

He inhales forcefully and exhales slowly. I also inhale, but mostly it's so I don't laugh at him.

"Yeah. Okay," he finally says. "I'll just… uh… I think I'm gonna play my game."

"You do that," I encourage and follow him out to the living room. "Just sit right there on the couch and get comfortable and I'll be back soon."

He follows my instructions, as if he's the one with cramps. I make a mental note to prepare myself in case someday he gets the man flu.

Once he's settled on the couch, I grab my keys and favorite Prada bag and head out the door. We finally picked up my car after Kade spent a week hauling me around. He says he doesn't mind, but he's already going above and beyond. I don't ever want him to feel like I'm taking advantage of him.

The store is only a mile or so away so it doesn't take

long to get there. It feels good to be out on my own again. I like shopping by myself. I don't like being rushed. I'd rather peruse the aisles a bit, check clearance racks for anything I might need, and read labels. It drives Kiersten nuts but she always has somewhere she has to be.

I park my car and grab a cart on my way in, just in case I find a bunch of things I can't live without. Taking a deep, relaxing breath, I just enjoy being out in the middle of life again. Sure, I may be at a crappy big box store but I'm still hearing the squeals of children and seeing the Halloween decorations all on display. It's my version of heaven.

My first stop is the clearance aisle to see what sales they have. It's usually hit or miss but this time, I was right to grab a cart. With summer over, I feel like I hit the jackpot—I snag some new water wings for Carson and a couple of pool noodles for just ten cents apiece. They even have a Paw Patrol character set on super sale that I can put away for Carson's Christmas present.

I scour the shelves for anything else of interest but don't find anything I need. Still, I call this visit a win.

Making my way to the feminine product aisles, my attention is on a giant jack-o-lantern blow up for someone's yard decoration so I don't notice until I'm practically next to him.

Jeremy.

He's here.

In the store.

In the Halloween section I'm walking through.

My heart begins racing and my breathing gets short. What is he doing here? Why is he still in town?

I grip the cart handle tightly as my mind races with the realization that he hasn't gone anywhere. It's then that I notice he's with a woman. A woman who touches his back lightly and smiles at him like he hung the moon.

Oh God. He's dating someone but he hasn't left either.

I will never leave you alone.

Visions from my nightmare flash before my eyes and it's all I can do to stay upright. I have to get out of here.

Before I can make a move, his body turns my way. It's as if he can feel my presence and knows he has me frozen in place. Then, he makes eye contact.

My blood runs cold as he flashes an evil grin and begins walking toward me. That's when my legs finally catch up with the rest of me and I quickly flee, abandoning my cart full of goodies.

It feels like every fifth step I'm turning around to make sure he's not following me. I'm sure I look like a crazy person and I have no doubt security will be pulling the tape to make sure I'm not a shoplifter, but I don't care. I need to get out of here as quickly as possible.

Jeremy is back and I won't feel safe again until I'm home with Kade. Even then, I'm not sure I'll ever feel safe again.

FOURTEEN
Kade

"I'm switching to pistols." Archie can't seem to figure out what kind of gun he wants to use today. He's been switching back and forth between pistols and a shotgun. I keep waiting for someone to take him out because of how indecisive he's being.

"What's your deal today?" Rodney's deep voice fills the headset. "You're acting like my wife trying to decide what to wear."

"I heard that!" comes a female voice in the background.

"Ooooh, you got caught…" we raze him and laugh while Rodney puts on his husband cap and says, "I'm sorry honey. You're right. Archie is just being a little bitch tonight."

"Hey!" Archie protests, but I murmur my agreement.

"It's true and you know it," Rodney defends. "I'm grateful I'm not partnered up with you in the real wild west or we'd already be dead."

"Asshole," Archie grumbles without a lot of weight behind his words.

"Check inside the saloon," I order, taking over since everyone else seems to be distracted. "Any sign of trouble in there?"

Rodney's avatar goes through the swinging doors, then gives us the all-clear.

"What'd I miss?" Matty asks, rejoining us after taking a few minutes away.

"Rodney got yelled at by his wife."

"Archie's pussing out." Our two gamer friends talk over the top of each other making me laugh as they piss each other off. It's been a weird night for play. But I didn't have anything else to do when Nicole left for the store so here I am, listening to everyone bitch each other out while we all play like shit.

"Where'd you go, anyway?" It's not like Matty to leave mid-game. Even the others know it. They've gotten quiet, probably waiting for his answer. Buncha gossips.

"I just grabbed an ice pack for my shoulder," Matty explains and reengages his avatar. "I got a nasty hit right in the shoulder cap the other day and it's not healing as fast as I'd like."

"Have you told the trainer? Gotten it checked out yet?"

"Hell no," he says forcefully. "They'd tell Coach who would pull me as a starter. And then my dad would get involved and you know how that would go. He'd freak out and take me across the country to some specialist he knows from back in the day and I'd spend hours getting scans and shit for them to say it's a sprain or something stupid. It's fine. Just taking a little longer than normal to heal."

"It's not fine, Matty," I argue, trying to be the voice of reason. "If you're still icing it days later, something is wrong. You're being scouted heavily. You've got to take care of yourself."

"Exactly. I'm being scouted. I don't need to miss a game over stupid shit." I know he's getting irritated with me but I've been around his family for a long time and I know this isn't something they would want him to mess with.

"Better you miss a game than have a career-ending injury before you even get a career."

"Why are you on me like this, man?" His avatar's movements become jerky. Either he's having issues because of his shoulder or he's more pissed than he's letting on. "Swear to God, if you don't let it go, I'm going to shoot you in the face."

"Do it and I'll call your dad to rat you out. See how well that goes over."

"You're a dick." Suddenly his avatar disappears leaving the three of us to battle it out again.

"Uhhh… that was intense, man," Rodney remarks, as he orders a drink at the bar.

"Trust me. That was the least of the drama in this family."

"Wait." Archie sounds confused and his avatar turns around to look at mine. It's kind of creepy. "You guys are family?"

"Yes. No. It's a long-ass story you don't want to know about. How do you think we both ended up on this game together?"

"Luck of the draw like the rest of us," Rodney says. He's got a point. I guess I can see why they're surprised. "You better order something, Archie, or you're going to get kicked out before we figure out what's coming next."

The red-headed avatar begins moving again and we're back on.

"Check out that dude dressed in the Zorro costume.

Does he look shady to you?" I ask, getting my own focus back into the game.

It only lasts for a matter of seconds before the front door slams behind me. Nicole never slams the door. She says she doesn't want to be a bad neighbor, which is why it has me immediately on edge. Every hair on my body feels like it's standing on end and I don't even have to turn around. I know instinctually something is very wrong.

Jumping up from the couch, I swivel on my heel to see Nicole leaning against the door, hand over her chest, a look of horror on her face.

Tossing my controller onto the couch, I race to her. "What? What's wrong?"

"He's here."

I take a quick step back, my hand clamped over my mouth as I take in what she just said.

"Jeremy?"

Just one word, said quietly, and her nod of confirmation makes the bottom drop out of my world again.

"Where?"

"I… I don't know." Her breathing is shallow. I approach her again and grab her hand, hoping to ground her so she doesn't pass out. "He was at the store."

"The one right around the corner?"

"Yes," she whispers, her eyes glistening with unshed tears.

"Shit."

"He was with a woman, Kade. He's dating someone." My first thought is that she's jealous. Upset that he's moved on. But then she grabs at my shirt, holding it tightly in her fist. "What if he's doing the same thing to her? We can't let him do that."

I'm not able to take the small space left over between

us anymore and pull her into a hug. Rubbing circles on her back, I do my best to help her process this new information. "Did you see any marks on her?"

I feel her head shake against my chest.

"Did she look frightened of him?"

Nicole pulls away and frightened blue eyes look up at me. "No. She looked really in love. That's the worst part. When he noticed me, he gave me this evil grin, like he knew he'd won. And she didn't even notice. How can she not see how dangerous he is? I don't know what to do."

My blood boils, knowing he's playing a game with Nicole. That he's just enough of a psychopath that he finds this fun. It's bad enough that he beat her, but to purposely make her afraid for his own entertainment is crossing yet another line.

I tamp down my own anger, though. This is not the time for me to go off the deep end, not when the woman I love is practically hyperventilating in front of me. Right now, I need to bottle up all my feelings and focus on her.

I rub my hands up and down her arms, hoping to soothe her. "Okay, okay, one thing at a time. Breathe with me, babe. Breathe in, two, three, four… and hold, two, three, four… out, two, three, four… hold, two, three, four."

It takes a few cycles of the technique I watched Kiersten do with her the last time she saw Jeremy, but her pants finally level out to a more normal pattern.

"Better?"

Nicole swallows and licks her lips before nodding. "Yeah. Yeah, thank you."

"We can't worry about the new girlfriend right now."

Her eyes widen. "But—" she tries to interrupt but I keep going.

"First we have to make sure you're protected and hope

that when she finds out about it, which she will at some point, it'll raise a red flag she can't ignore."

"But what if he hurts her tonight?"

I hate that Nicole is panicking over this, but I so much admire that she's less worried about herself than she is about another person. Although I suspect part of it is actually a defense mechanism so she doesn't have to address her own fear.

"Do you know her name?"

"Well… no," she admits.

"Do you know where she lives?"

Nicole shakes her head, lips twisted into a frown.

"I want to help her as much as you do, but without any of that information, we don't even have a place to start."

Nicole's shoulders drop, her forehead resting on my chest as she speaks. "I just can't stand the idea that it could be happening right now and there's nothing I can do to stop him."

"I know. But I really think she'll be okay tonight."

"How can you say that." Her head whips up so she can look at me again, but she doesn't pull away. Her fist is still clamped around my shirt like I'm her lifeline. I have no complaints about it. "How can you be so sure?"

"He's kind of a psychopath, Nic. And right now, he's feeling awfully in control since he scared you at the store. I don't know a lot about human psychology but I've known quite a few assholes in my life and usually when they feel in control like this, they just sort of sit back and gloat. It's when they're losing control that they're dangerous."

Nicole's brows furrow and I can tell she's considering my words. I don't know for sure that I'm right, but like her, I hope I am.

"Yeah," she finally says, still gazing off into her own

thoughts. "That makes sense. I hope you're right."

"Me, too." Spontaneously, I kiss her on the top of the head and guide her toward the couch. I'll take the time to think harder about kissing her later. Right now, I just want to get her settled.

"Oh, shoot," she exclaims as I gently push her down onto the cushion. "I didn't get my tampons."

"I can go get them." I'm planning on leaving to set some things in motion anyway, but I don't tell her that part. "Why don't you play *Red Dead Redemption*? The guys are on right now."

"Okay." Her answer is a little too robotic for my liking. I make a mental note to be on my guard tonight for when the nightmares start.

Grabbing the headset, I hop back on real quick.

"Hey, guys, I gotta head out but I'm handing things over to Nicole."

"What the fuck is happening tonight, Maxwell?" Rodney bitches. "First Archie fumbling everything up—"

"You're a dick," Archie heckles.

"—Then Matty pusses out. And now you're just ditching us?"

"I have some things to take care of. Besides, you like playing with Nicole more than you like playing with me anyway."

"She's definitely hotter than you," Archie butts in.

"You don't know what either of us looks like, asshole," I reply and then think better of it. "But now that you say it, yeah, that's true. Even in avatar form."

They both start laughing as I sign off.

"Here she is, y'all."

Ripping the headset off, I hand it and the controller to Nicole. "You can sign in if you want or you can just keep playing me. I have more weapons built up than you do, so if you want to play around with them you can."

"Sweet, thanks."

Her response is almost normal, which is a little disconcerting. She just came from a huge scare and seems to be recovering from it way too quickly. She doesn't even seem concerned about my leaving her alone.

Yeah, something's not right.

Once she's settled, I go into the hall bathroom and search under the cabinets for what I need. Ripping the tops off the only two boxes of feminine products I find, I shove them in my pocket so I know what I'm looking for. Then I grab my keys off the counter in the kitchen.

Taking one last look at Nicole to make sure she's settled, I feel confident she's okay with me leaving which is weird, but works to my benefit right now. She needs supplies and I need some privacy.

I shut the door quietly behind me as I leave, making sure all the locks are engaged. As I race to my car, needing to get back to her as quickly as possible, I pull out my phone, search for the contact I need, and dial.

It takes just two rings before I get an answer. "What's up, Kade."

"Paul. We have a problem."

FIFTEEN
Nicole

"**Y**ou didn't have to come with me."

I purse my lips and raise one eyebrow at my sister who insisted on escorting me to my therapy appointment. It was luck that I happened to have my regular biweekly appointment today. With all the drama last night, the timing was undeniably perfect.

Kiersten is not at all threatened by my glare. "Yes, I did. He's out there and, full disclosure, I'm almost as terrified as you're pretending not to be."

I gape at her, hating that she can read me so well. I thought I was doing a decent job of hiding my feelings. "I am not terrified…"

She flashes the same look at me that I was giving her. The one that says, *You're full of it.*

I sigh and give up the ruse. "Fine. How can you tell?"

"Nicole, you have been my sister for your entire life. You're naturally a quiet person. But when you get too calm, I know things are heavy on you. It's obvious to everyone who knows you that you are really shaken by this.

I'm surprised Kade hasn't had a meltdown yet from how worried he is."

That's twice she's surprised me in the last thirty seconds. "Kade is worried too? He's been so nonchalant."

Kiersten snorts a humorless laugh. "Why do you think he called Paul last night and not me? Because he's gone into full-on alpha protective mode and was rallying the troops."

"Whatever." I settle back into the couch because I know she's wrong about this. "He called Paul to give him a heads up because Paul is like my brother and he's passing on information."

She points right in my face. "Wrong. That boy is head over heels, madly in love with you and he's freaking out because none of us know what Jeremy is up to and he's desperate to protect you. Even if it means getting his boss involved."

I can feel the blood draining from my face, her words a shock. "No, he's not. Maybe he has a little crush. But mostly he's my friend."

"Yeah, a friend who would love benefits." She sits forward and turns to face me. "Do you not notice how he looks at you? He is in *looooooooove*, Nic," she singsongs. "And don't think I don't know that you're madly in love with him, too. You both think we're all idiots."

My eyes widen and my jaw drops. "Everyone else knows, too?"

"You aren't exactly sneaky when you steal glances and blush. We just didn't say anything because we didn't want to embarrass you." She flops back and stretches her long legs out, like she's exhausted from the bombshell she just dropped. Then she turns her head toward me. "And for the record, I give you my blessing. He's a great guy and I think he's exactly what you need."

My lips quirk up as I fight the smile that wants to take over. I was starting to think Kade liked me a little, but in love with me? How can that be? I barely have a job, I'm a college dropout, and I still carry around the scars of an abusive relationship. How could he possibly feel that deeply for me?

Then again, I wouldn't be upset if he did. He's such a great person and underneath the geeky gamer exterior is a heart of gold. I just wish he could see himself the way I do.

"Anyway, after we're done here, I'll take you back to Kade's and since Kade is off tonight, Paul will pick you up for work."

"I have my own car, Kiersten. Is carting me around everywhere really necessary?"

"Yeah," she says a little more forcefully than I care for. "It's absolutely necessary at this point and I have no idea why you keep bucking me on this. We don't know what Jeremy is up to and I'm not leaving you alone to find out. And you're definitely not leaving Kade's apartment by yourself anymore."

"Glad you're making decisions about my life now." I cross my arms indignantly, like the child I apparently am.

"Oh, I'm sorry. I thought we didn't want the guy who beat you and put you in the hospital to get near you again. My mistake." Her voice is dripping with sarcasm. I already know I've lost this battle. I just hate when she's right sometimes. "Do you want me to drop you back at the bar apartment so you can be all alone with your thoughts again?"

"No," I admit begrudgingly. I don't know why I'm so resistant. I'm just… irritated by it all. Just when I started getting my life back, it feels like it's being snatched away again.

"Exactly. So, let me be your big sister and help take care of you."

"Is this how it's going to be now? Are you guys going to rotate who gets to babysit me in public for the foreseeable future?"

Kiersten huffs her irritation with me. "Stop being obstinate. If there's something in particular you do or don't want us to do, speak up. But until you start voicing your thoughts, this is what you get."

I sigh in resignation because she's right. I'm kind of frozen. Instead of facing my fears head-on, I'm ignoring them and stuffing them down more and more. I know it's not healthy and will backfire on me eventually but I wasn't expecting to see Jeremy again. I was doing a good job healing and I don't want to start all over. And yet, I'm hiding out in Kade's apartment instead of doing something to actually fix the problem, so how much healing have I really been doing?

It's a good thing I have therapy. There are a few things I may need help sorting out.

Right on time, the door opens and Dr. Rhonda pokes her head out.

"Hi Nicole." One of the things that I like about Dr. Rhonda is she always starts our session with a smile. Even if we dig into the deep stuff, I always know she'll let me get comfortable being here before we do the heavy work. "Are you ready?"

I follow her into the small office and take a seat at the end of the couch, curling my feet up next to me and clutching the small decorative pillow. I sit in this position every time. Dr. Rhonda says it's normal and is a defensive position. It gives me a sense of control so we can do the hard work. I don't know if that's true, but I'm much more comfortable sitting right here, just like this.

"How are you doing today?" Dr. Rhonda sits in her office chair across from me, her dark red hair pulled back into a casual chignon. She likes to gently swivel back and forth while we talk and she never takes notes during our sessions. I like that about her. It makes me feel like I'm having a conversation and not being psychoanalyzed. Realistically, I know she's still doing her job and probably writing things down after the fact, but for me, it's helpful to feel like I'm just talking to a friend.

"I'm okay." It's not quite the truth, but not a lie either.

"Last week, you were still living with… Kade? Is that his name?"

I nod. "Kade, yes."

"Things had kind of calmed down since your mother's unexpected visit and you hadn't heard from Jeremy."

"Yeah, well he's around." I run my fingers through the fringe on my favorite pillow, calming myself. "I ran into him at the store last night."

Her chair stops swiveling and I know she wasn't expecting that news. "How did it go when you saw him?"

I blow out a breath, gathering my thoughts. I want to downplay it all—convince her of how strong I am. But I don't feel strong and Kiersten's right, I'm not being honest with anyone, least of all myself. This is the safest place to let my guard down and I have to do it if I'm ever going to heal completely.

"It was terrifying." I think back to the moment he realized I was watching him, allowing all the details to come into focus. "He gave me this… smile, like he knew what he was doing to me, how I was feeling this intense fear and it's what he wanted. He wanted me to be afraid. But that's not likely right?"

I want her to agree with me. If she does, it means everyone has overreacted. More than anything I want that to be the case. Overreaction means I'm safer than everyone thinks. I also know better than to think Dr. Rhonda is going to give me the answer I want to hear.

"Depends on the person. Some abusers just snap and feel some form of remorse later. Others find it to be a game. There's no way I can know for sure. Best way to proceed, though, is to listen to your gut with this." My shoulders slouch. That's not what I wanted to hear because I know exactly what my gut says.

She leans forward, placing her elbows on her knees. "My question for you is, how does the situation make you feel?"

"Completely out of control." I realize that's the first time I've said it out loud. But I'm so tired of hiding. I can feel the frustration beginning to bubble to the surface and my words aren't far behind. "I'm always looking over my shoulder and my nightmares are back in full force so I can't even escape him when I'm sleeping. And don't get me started on my family. They're great and I know they're just trying to help but it's so annoying having my sister and her boyfriend babysitting me all the time. Oh, and that doesn't include their friends. I already know what's about to happen. There's going to be a rotation of guys who think they're bouncers at the bar every time I work keeping an eye out for me."

"Is that such a bad thing right now?"

Automatically, my mouth opens to say *yes, yes it's a bad thing*, but I stop myself.

"No," I admit quietly. "It's really nice that I have so many people who love me. I just… I just wish I could protect myself."

"Why can't you?"

I worry my lip for a few minutes, my thoughts spinning. There may be a way I can take my power back, I just don't know if I'm strong enough yet. Then again, maybe Dr. Rhonda would be able to help me figure it out.

"I was kind of thinking… I don't know if maybe it's too late and I can't do it or something. It was just a thought." I rub my fingers together nervously as I consider whether I can even say it out loud.

"What kind of thought?"

I still hesitate. What if I'm wrong? What if I can't do this?

"We're just talking Nicole," Dr. Rhonda soothes. "Tossing around ideas to see what might work. There's no commitment on your part at this point."

That's true. I don't have to do anything. I can just ask her about it. No one has to know. "I was wondering if maybe I could get a protection order or something. Do you think I could do that so he'd have to stay away from me?"

"Sure." She sits up again, her chair beginning to move. "I think that might be a good idea. It gives you a little peace of mind, but also gives you some legal recourse."

"Okay."

"Have you inquired about one yet?"

"No. I don't even know who to call. It wasn't in this county so do I call them or call someone here? Does it cost money? I have no idea where to begin."

"I'm sure you could call the police non-emergency line and someone could give you the information on where to start. Again, there's no pressure to follow through. Just gather the information first so you can make an informed decision."

She stands up from her chair and grabs her phone off

the desk. "Would you like me to look up the phone number? Again, you don't have to use it, but it's one less thing you have to sort out if you decide to call."

I take a deep breath and nod quickly before I can change my mind. There's no harm in just asking some questions, right? It would never even get back to him. I think.

I'm terrified of what the fallout might mean if I decide to pursue a restraining order. But as I think about it, I realize that the fear of pursuing an order of protection is more acute because it's immediate. The fear of not knowing when he'll show up or what he might say runs deep down into my soul, lingering and showing up at random times.

It's like the difference between cutting my finger with a knife and breaking my finger. The knife hurts, but it heals relatively quickly and then it's over and done with, a scar left in its place but one that fades over time, never to be thought of again.

On the other hand, a break seems never-ending and even leaves some phantom pains behind that come up regularly.

I don't want that. I'd rather the knife because I want to never have to think of Jeremy again.

Mind made up, I gratefully take the sticky note from Dr. Rhonda when she hands it to me. Looking at her meticulous cursive writing, I realize my decision is made.

It's time for me to take back my control, for myself and any other woman he decides is his next target. I know exactly what I have to do.

SIXTEEN
Kade

In true "my luck" fashion, I got stuck working on Halloween, which means we have to dress in costume today. I went the easy route and asked Jaxon to borrow some scrubs so I could pretend to be a doctor. Suddenly, I understand the appeal of wearing this uniform. It's like I'm wearing pajamas at work.

The downside is the pants are thin and if I spill, I may become the world's worst wet t-shirt contestant. But the comfort level makes it worth it.

Tammy came dressed as the Bride of Frankenstein and even I have to admit she looks amazing. I knew she had thick hair, but I had no idea how much of it there is until she stuck it all up straight. I don't know if she thinks there's a costume contest later, but she'd win if there was.

She's also overly happy to have a packed house tonight. Her laughter has filled the room since the doors opened, enjoying all the costumes and dropping "treats" on the tables for her favorite customers. They love it.

If I'd known a mini Snickers could make some of these

guys tip better, I would have brought some long ago.

"Hey, Kade. We are running low on glow sticks." Nicole's dark-rimmed eyes startle me even though I've been looking at them for hours. She decided to come as a zombie, complete with ripped clothing, a pale face with dark-rimmed eyes, and hair that I'm pretty sure she never brushed today.

She's the prettiest zombie I've ever seen. Except those eyes that keep freaking me out.

"I'm going to grab some from the back while we're slow."

Slow is a relative term, but at least we don't have a line at the bar anymore.

"Sure. Go ahead. And can you see if we have any more dry ice back there? I've made more Swamp Sippers than I expected."

"Sure."

She takes off to the back, patting Frankie on the arm as she walks by. He's been hanging out on a stool, drinking water and watching Sports Center all night. Unless the door opens. Then he stares down anyone who walks in. It makes me feel better knowing he's here in case there's trouble.

I continue to mix and pour, Tammy taking orders left and right. Even with our specialty drinks today, it feels like mindless work. Mindless enough that I have time to think about how Nicole seems different today. Lighter. It's like something shifted with her since her therapy appointment the other day. I don't ask because it's not my business, but whatever it was, I'm grateful to her therapist for it.

The door opens and a couple dressed as what I think is Abbott and Costello walks in and takes a seat at one of the high-top tables. Frankie glares at them, then determines they're harmless and goes back to Sports Center. Without missing a beat, Tammy is taking their order.

Tucker Hayes sits down at the bar at the same time, an almost full beer in his hand. He's one of the few here who didn't dress up for the holiday. Unless you consider the ball cap hiding his floppy hair as dressing up.

"Hey man," I greet without slowing down on my mixing. "Having a good time?"

Tucker smiles as he glances around the room. "I am. I wasn't sure what to expect tonight, but everyone in costume and creepy music wasn't it."

"We're just trying to be festive tonight. Bring a little magic to the day. Have you tried one of the Halloween drinks? Even I have to admit it's kind of cool seeing the dry ice do its magic."

Tucker takes a swig of his beer. "I've seen them but I think I'll stick with this. I feel like those things may be more fun to look at than drink."

We both watch as I drop the last ingredient into the drink I'm mixing and smoke begins pouring over the lip of the glass. I've seen a few people cough while trying not to breathe in the smoke.

"Can I get you another beer then?"

"Sure." He begins peeling the label off his bottle and I have the distinct impression he's trying to build up some nerve. I'm just not sure for what.

"Can I ask you a question?" he finally asks, my curiosity piqued after several long seconds of silence from him.

"Hit me." I place the last of Tammy's orders on a fresh tray so she can just grab them and go, then turn my attention to Tucker. "What's up?"

"Is she taken?"

My eyebrows raise along with my defenses because I

know exactly who he's talking about. But I play dumb. I need to hear him say it out loud just in case I'm overreacting.

"Come on, man. You know who I'm talking about," he pleads. I've never seen him nervous like this. Normally Tucker is the life of the party. I don't like that he's interested enough to be nervous about asking. But I won't let him wuss out either. If he's going to try to pursue Nicole, she deserves for him to man up.

Finally, he relents, knowing I'm not giving him even an inch. "Nicole. Is Nicole single?"

"She's not available, man."

The words are out before I can stop them. I didn't intend to sound rude, nor did I intend to fudge the truth. But I can't help how possessive I feel over her.

My harsh tone wasn't missed by Tucker who looks taken aback. "Oh sorry, man. I didn't realize you guys were together."

"We're not."

He squeezes his eyes shut and then opens them, his brows furrowed in confusion. "But you said she's not available? Wait. Is she a lesbian?"

I roll my eyes. Such a stereotype to assume a woman who is unavailable to date must be gay. "No. Just… there's a lot happening right now. Leave her alone okay?"

"Does this have anything to do with what happened that night?"

I had forgotten Tucker was here when Jeremy showed up. It makes sense that he would finally put it together. I know I'm crossing a line with the conversation, but knowing someone else is interested in her, someone who can give her everything she deserves, is like a stab right in my heart. With that feeling overwhelming me, I give him another half-truth.

"Yes." The air shifts and I feel her slide back behind the counter. Glancing over my shoulder, I see her putting a new bag of glow sticks on the shelf behind us. Turning back to Tucker, I lower my volume. "Give her some time to work through all of that, okay?"

Tucker nods his response and immediately flashes a giant smile as Nicole approaches.

"Hey Nicole. Nice Zombie outfit."

She smiles right back at him, oblivious to the conversation she just walked in on. "Hi Tucker. Nice... normal clothes you've got on."

I place the fresh beer in front of him. "Yeah, I'm not a huge Halloween fan."

"Too bad. I just brought out some brand-new glow sticks. Maybe if you're nice, I'll give you one just so you can be part of the party."

"I can hardly wait," he says sarcastically as she turns to me.

"I didn't find any more dry ice, but it might be in the liquor closet..."

Her words taper off and the bottle of beer she was holding drops to the floor, shattering glass and liquid everywhere. Her face pales to a shade lighter than the makeup she's wearing and she looks like she's seen a ghost. I grab her arm, steadying her. "What's wrong?"

It's then that I notice she can't take her eyes off at the couple that just came in, Abbott and Costello. I look at them a little closer and the realization hits me out of nowhere.

"That's him isn't it?"

She nods and takes a step back.

Frankie looks up and I gesture to him, hoping he understands my signal.

I feel so stupid. I've seen Jeremy before. I should know what he looks like. But the last time he was here, it all happened so fast, in my mind his facial features are fuzzy.

But now that the breaking bottle has caught that asshole's attention and he's facing this way, I recognize the cocky air around him. I want to wipe that arrogant smirk off his face. He's here specifically so he can terrorize Nicole on purpose. I know it and he knows it.

Anger surges through my veins, but I'm not the only one.

"Which one." Frankie doesn't ask. He demands an answer and I have no problem giving it to him.

Gesturing with my head so I don't have to let Nicole go, I give Frankie what he wants. "The guy who just walked in sitting at the high top table with the brunette. Abbott and Costello."

Frankie stalks off, Tucker flanking him. It's then that I notice several others have stood up, all recognizing something serious is going down. They're not my concern, though. Nicole is.

Turning back to her, I run my hands down her arms, her touch calming my own nerves. It's like a constant reminder that she's still here in front of me, since my adrenaline seems to still be unconvinced. "Are you okay?"

My heart breaks when she shakes her head.

"What can I do? Anything. Tell me and I'll do whatever it takes to make this better."

"Nothing," she says, refusing to take her eyes off the man of her nightmares. "There's nothing you can do, Kade. I'm the only one who can stop this."

Her body shakes beneath my hand, though her voice has an eerie calm to it.

I take one step closer. "What does that mean?"

"You can't kick me out every time, Nicole!" a voice suddenly yells from across the room. "I live here now! I have a right to be in public places even if you don't want me around!"

I want to jump over the counter and punch Jeremy in the face to knock him down a few pegs, but Frankie's got it covered. He pushes the asshole, making him stumble. "Get out of here, man. This is a private establishment and you aren't welcome here."

"Don't fucking touch me, douchebag."

Jeremy gets right in Frankie's face, like he's ready to fight. Frankie bucks up to him, not threatened at all. He has a few inches on Jeremy, but the important part is how much broader he is. Jeremy may be big compared to the women he likes to date, but Frankie would pummel him and he knows it. When Tucker takes a step closer too, standing next to Frankie with arms crossed over broad shoulders, Jeremy knows he's lost this battle before it even began.

Whoever the woman is, she grabs at Jeremy's arm. "Please, baby. Let's just go, okay? There are other bars and parties, right? Please."

It's clear he's trying to decide how to get out of this with his pride intact, but he'll get no help from anyone here. Finally, he backs down.

"Whatever man," he spits out as he takes a few steps back. "This place is a shit hole anyway." Glancing around the room, he sees all eyes on him and decides for one last dig. "Watch yourself after drinking anything that dirty whore makes." He points right at Nicole but has the smarts to keep moving. "You don't where she's been. I know the shit she's done. I've seen it with my own eyes."

Nicole gasps but I pull her closer to me, as if I can protect her from his harsh words.

"Better walk faster, asshole, before I have to help you out the door," Frankie threatens. I know he doesn't want to fight, that his coach wouldn't be happy if he showed up at practice with a black eye. But I also know it's a sacrifice he's willing to make if necessary.

Fortunately, Jeremy knows it too. "Let's go," he says to the woman who takes one last look at everyone, obviously confused by where all the bad blood has come from. And yet, she follows him.

As soon as the door closes behind them, the tension begins to disappear from the bar, customers happily returning to their good time at Tammy's insistence.

Back here, it's a different story. "Really, are you okay?"

I'm surprised she's still standing upright but to her credit, Nicole's breathing is steady and there is a fire in her eyes I haven't seen before.

"I'm fine. I know what I have to do."

I don't know what that means, but from the resolve on her face, she's ready to get it done.

SEVENTEEN
Nicole

should have worn layers. Police stations are always cold.

Or maybe they aren't, but my body can't stop shaking and I just think I'm cold.

Or maybe it's nerves.

Either way, I could use an extra layer of warmth to help steady me because I'm so nervous I can hardly stand it.

I know coming here is the right thing to do. I have to take some steps for my own personal safety, but that doesn't mean it doesn't scare me so badly I want to run away. I won't though. I refuse. I need to get this done.

My sister's hand suddenly covers mine and squeezes. I grab onto her for dear life, thankful she knows how hard this is and is here to help me through it.

"Thanks for coming with me." My words are practically a whisper, as if I don't want anyone to hear me speaking. I know it's irrational to think that way, but somehow it feels disrespectful to make any noise in this place where people might help me.

"Of course, I'm here with you," she responds at a much more normal volume. "I wouldn't leave you to do this alone."

"I know. But I wasn't exactly nice when you went with me to my therapy appointment."

"No, you weren't," she agrees, making my stomach churn with guilt. Kiersten has never done anything but try to support me. "But I understood why you were irritable. You feel like everything is out of control right now. I know how frustrating that is. I used to be the same way with Heath and Lauren."

I turn to look at her more closely. This is news to me. "You were?"

"Oh yeah," she says dismissively like this is old news. "They would make decisions for me all the time. It drove me crazy that Heath found a daycare for Carson and wanted to pay for it. Like I couldn't do it on my own."

"What made you finally stop being pissy about it?"

"I realized I *couldn't* do it on my own. My issue wasn't so much about him doing things as much as my own pride over the fact that I wasn't able to without them. I needed their help and they were doing it graciously and with no expectation of me ever being able to return the favor." She shrugs and looks at me imploringly. "It was just because they loved us. When I realized that part, everything shifted. They gave me one less thing I had to stress about and I was able to let it go and just say thank you."

I give my sister a weak smile and squeeze her hand again. "I get it. Thank you."

She squeezes back and nudges my shoulder with hers. "You're welcome."

We both look up as someone approaches – a female officer stands in front of us, hands on her utility belt. "Nicole

Willoughby?"

"Yes, ma'am." I stand up faster than I intend, forcing her to take two steps back. My eyes widen in embarrassment.

Kiersten immediately stands next to me, although slower than I did, and puts her arm around me reassuringly. "Hey. Calm down. We're just here for you to ask questions."

I blow out a quick breath, making sure I don't hyperventilate. "Sorry. I just… yes, that's me."

The officer smiles at us kindly. "I'm Officer Hanson and she's right. I'm here to help you with whatever it is you're inquiring about. Care to step into my office?"

I nod a little too quickly but she doesn't seem put off by my nerves. If anything, Officer Hanson seems used to dealing with nervous women like me. I'm not sure if that makes me feel better or makes me sad that so many of us come to talk to her.

She leads us through a small maze of hallways before taking us into a small office. It seems pretty typical—white walls, small wooden desk with two plastic chairs in front of it, bookshelf off to the right full of manuals and various police trinkets. Shutting the door, Officer Hanson takes a seat in a swivel office chair, not noticing the squeak it makes when she sits.

"How can I help you ladies?" She glances back and forth at us, her eyes eventually falling to me.

I lick my bottom lip before speaking. "I was told you might be able to help me get a protection order against my ex-boyfriend."

To her credit, Officer Hanson doesn't so much as flinch, just nods in understanding. "I can definitely give you information about that. Can I ask why you feel you are in danger?"

I suck in a quick breath and glance at my sister who gives me a reassuring nod. "He used to hit me."

"I'm sorry to hear that." Her tone remains unchanged. I had no idea how much I would appreciate that. Most people who find out I used to be in an abusive situation give me looks that can only be described as pity. But she's treating it very matter of fact. I suppose in her line of work, this is not an unusual conversation.

Officer Hanson grabs a pen off her desk and flips a clean sheet of paper onto her notebook. "Did you ever file a report about the abuse?"

I shake my head, suddenly furious at myself for not taking a stand before. "I was afraid. Partly of him and partly for him." I glance down at the floor as the realization hits me. "Wow. I never put that together before."

"Can I ask why you were afraid for him?"

I look back up at her, half expecting her to think I'm an idiot because of my answer. "I knew he'd lose his scholarship and I didn't want his college career to end because of me."

Glancing away, I shake my head at my own stupidity. How ridiculous that I let the man who put me in the hospital get away with abusing me because I was afraid for *his* life. What about *mine*? Why did I put him first?

"Ms. Willoughby?" My eyes snap back over to the officer, whose expression remains unchanged. "This is nothing to be upset about. Your answer is neither uncommon nor unrealistic in domestic violence situations. Many times, it takes months or even years of being distant from the situation to see things a little more clearly. Domestic violence is tightly wrapped up with emotional abuse. It's why so many people never get away from their abuser. But you did. That's the important part."

Kiersten grabs my hand again and places it on her lap, clasping it tightly. My eyes fall closed and I take a few moments to take a deep breath and refocus on the task at hand.

When I finally look up again, I give her a nod, ready to continue.

Officer Hanson writes something down and begins asking questions. "You said he's your ex-boyfriend."

"Yes, ma'am."

"May I have his name and any personal information you have on him?"

I answer as much as I can, which isn't much—name, birth date, and last known address are all I have. She writes it all down, but the hard part isn't over. There are still details to share that I've never discussed with anyone. Not even my sister.

"I reserve judgment on any case I look into until I gather all the facts, so please don't think I'm insensitive to the situation. However, if you move forward with this, a judge is going to ask you all this and more. So, I need to know why now? If you aren't together and haven't been for a while, why do you think you need protection from him?"

"I moved here to get away from him. I thought he was gone for good, but recently he's found me. And he's shown up at my work a couple of times already."

Her eyebrow moves up a fraction of an inch, but I see it. I'm not sure what it means, though.

"He didn't know where you had moved?"

"I'm sure he assumed I was with my sister. I mean, my mom knew and she's… well… let's just say she's not very supportive when it comes to going against anyone associated with the ladies at the club." My lips twist in disgust just saying it out loud. Then I continue. "Anyway, my mom came to visit a few weeks ago and she brought him with her. Now he won't leave. He comes into the bar where I work to just stare at me. And I saw him at the store. He was with some girl and he just smiled at me like he knew I was afraid."

I puff out a breath having run out of steam. Officer Hanson, on the other hand, leans back in her chair. She tosses her pen on the desk and settles in. "I'm going to be perfectly honest here. We can file for a protection order, but without any record of you filing charges it's his word against yours."

My heart sinks, but Kiersten jumps in quickly. "Well, wait. She didn't press charges, but he was arrested for assault when he put her in the hospital. The charges were dropped because at the time she was too afraid to testify."

Officer Hanson leans forward and grabs her pen again to jot down more notes. "You don't happen to have the case number, do you?"

Kiersten smirks victoriously. "Case number and the contact information of one of the officers who was involved in the case. Would that help?"

"It would help a lot actually. I assume it wasn't in this county?"

"No." Kiersten continues to answer her questions, handing her a small piece of paper that I assume is everything Officer Hanson needs. "This all happened in a suburb of Houston."

"And when was this?" Her pen moves frantically across the page.

"About a year ago."

Office Hanson finally finishes writing and leans back in her chair again, rocking briefly. "Let me ask you a question." She gives me a pointed look. "Would you be willing to testify against him now?"

I glance at Kiersten, my heartbeat picking up pace, before turning my attention back to her. "I think so. I mean I'd have to think about it for a little bit, but isn't it too late?"

"Statute of limitations in Texas for domestic assault is three years. If he's waiting for a trial, your protection order request will hold more weight."

"Nicole," my sister says gently, likely recognizing my inner turmoil. "You don't have to do this alone."

"I know it's just… a trial."

Officer Hanson's chair squeaks as she leans forward once again and crosses her arms on her desk. "I'm going to level with you, Ms. Willoughby. You said he's been with some other woman, right?"

I give her a quick nod, not sure what she's getting at.

"That's concerning to me. You may have been the first one he hurt, but the statistics show you won't be the last. I know you have a lot to think through, but this time it's not just about protecting yourself. This time it's about protecting other women, too." She raises her hands defensively. "That's not to say it's your responsibility to protect her. It's not. But if you're on the fence about it, maybe that'll give you the information you need to help make your decision."

I glance away as I process her words. She's right. Seeing him with another woman freaked me out, not because I miss him but because I know she's in danger. I know she's the only one who can make a choice for herself, but there's something I can do to make sure she has all the information. And not just her, but any woman he puts his sights on.

Taking a deep breath, I turn back to Officer Hanson, mind made up.

It's time. It's time I take my life back, and that means I

have to take part of his away.

"I'm ready. I want to press charges."

She taps the table with her fingers. "I'll put in the call to the arresting officer and get the process started. I have to warn you, the DA may not want to pursue it. But in light of this new information, we have a decent shot."

"I understand. Whatever you have to do is fine with me."

"Nicole," Kiersten says. "Are you one hundred percent sure? No going back."

"Absolutely," I say with more resolve than I've felt in an entire year. "I'm ready to have him out of my life for good. Whatever it takes."

EIGHTEEN
Kade

For the first time in however long, I'm sitting on my couch not playing video games. Instead, I'm humoring Nicole and watching some reality show about people on the internet. It's not as cringeworthy as I expected it to be. But that may be attributed to the fact that my thoughts are racing faster than the show is moving.

I really want to know how it went at the police station today. All Nicole told me is that she's ready to press charges on Jeremy. And then she turned on the television and the only thing we've talked about since is the show.

I don't want to pressure her into telling me anything she doesn't want to, but I feel like I've been left with the biggest cliffhanger in history.

I went to the police station. The end.

But I keep trying to focus on the show instead of demanding answers. It's not working out all that well.

"How many countries have done this reality show anyway?" I ask, going for a titillating conversation starter at least.

Nicole shrugs. "I don't know. The US, France, Brazil, or something. I don't care. As long as they keep making *The Circle*, I'll keep watching it."

"I admit it's not the worst reality show I've seen."

She bumps me with her shoulder. "You love it and you know it."

I prop my feet up on the coffee table. Knowing us, we'll be here for a while. "I can admit I see the appeal. At least it's not those crazy housewife ladies who throw shit at each other."

She giggles and goes back to watching. I'm not really paying that much attention. Right now it's a lot of reading messages back and forth. It's not that the conversations are boring, it's that my mind is just somewhere else. Mainly, the police station. But apparently, I'm not as good at hiding my curiosity as I think.

"You want to know how it went at the police station don't you?"

I drop my head and arms back with relief. I'm sure it looks like I've melted into the couch, which I probably have, so relieved she's the one who started the conversation. "Am I that obvious?"

"No," she replies with a giggle. "But I was kind of waiting to see how long it took until you broke and finally asked me about it."

I squeeze her knee, making her jump. "That's not very nice."

"I have very little entertainment these days," she says nonchalantly, then sits up and faces me. Situating herself so she's criss-cross, I have the impression this is about to be an intense conversation. My guard is immediately up as I sit up straight. "I am filing for the protection order, but I also agreed to let them reopen my case."

Her words are out in a rush, but don't give me much information.

"What does that mean?"

Nicole looks down at her lap, fidgeting with a stray string on her pant leg. "That means Jeremy is probably going to be arrested again, only this time I'll be testifying against him about what happened and he might get an assault conviction."

I open my mouth to respond, but then what she's *not* saying hits me. "You said he's *probably* going to get arrested."

"Yes."

"And he *might* get a conviction."

"Also, yes."

"Explain that part."

She drops the string and puffs out her cheeks before slowly pushing the air out. "It's up to the DA if they want to try again. Since I didn't exactly cooperate with them the last time they tried to throw the book at him, there's no guarantee they'll want to pursue it."

"But he's harassing you."

She smiles kindly at me, and I know it's her attempt at calming me down before I get too riled up. It just unnerves me that no one seems to take this as seriously as they should. She's so precious and they keep letting her down.

"I know. And the fact that he keeps showing up at work will hopefully be to our advantage. The lady officer we talked to today is going to try and convince them that I'm ready this time and there is a real need to finally give him some jail time."

"So, she thinks he'll go to jail?"

"I don't know. As far as I know, it was his first offense

so they might go lenient on him."

Again, I don't understand how the powers that be can just let this slide by. "But you were hurt badly."

"I know I was. But you know how it goes, Kade. He gets a good attorney who argues he's never done anything like this before and his white, country club parents show up dressed nice and the judge falls for the whole poor little rich boy act. I'm prepared for that."

I close my eyes briefly, gathering my thoughts. I'm angry, but more than that, I want to be here for her. To help her through this. "If you know it's a long shot, why do it?"

She glances away momentarily before answering. "To make sure he's not allowed to come near me for a very long time. And to maybe help that girl he's hanging out with."

"You know that's not your job right? You don't have to poke this bear or whatever for someone else's sake. You don't even know that anything is happening to her."

Her smile is small and forced and I feel like I've touched a nerve. "No, I don't know anything is happening to her yet. But it will. Maybe if he's arrested and convicted, she'll take this chance to get far away from him."

I suddenly realize, this is the first time I've heard Nicole talk about this whole issue without hesitation. It's also the first time it's come up at all without her looking like she's on the verge of a panic attack. It gives me this odd sense of pride. "Why do you seem really strong and resolved about this?"

"I don't know. I guess I just started looking around at all the support I get from my friends and family, and realized he can't hurt me anymore unless I let him. I don't want to let him anymore."

"I'm really glad you have that support system."

She leans forward and puts her hand on my knee. A shot of electricity runs straight to my dick. Maybe there will never be a time that it's appropriate to be so affected by the warmth of her skin, but now is definitely not the time to let her touch affect me.

Looking into my eyes, she tilts her head slightly. "You know you're part of that, right?"

Sucked into the deep look she's giving me, I can only answer with, "I am?"

"Of course. I feel… calm when I'm with you. You just make me feel peaceful."

"I do?"

She nudges me again playfully and I realize I'm barely able to put together sentences with her touching me. Fortunately, and also unfortunately, she removes her hand from my leg.

"Yes, silly. Remember that night you climbed in bed with me when I was having that nightmare?"

I've never forgotten it. I made mental notes of how her skin felt and how her body curved. I barely slept. I don't tell her any of that, though. "Yeah."

"I didn't dream at all that night. Nothing I can remember anyway. You make me feel peaceful."

I'd prefer it if I made her feel horny, but I'll take what I can get, even if it's a friend zone for now. I swallow hard at the thought.

"Well good. I'm glad I can be a good friend like that."

A strange look crosses her face before she moves away from me and turns her whole body so she faces the television again. The air shifts around us and I get the feeling I've said something wrong.

"What?" I ask, feeling a small desperation to fix whatever I just broke. "What did I say?"

Nicole worries her bottom lip, like she's battling herself and how much she wants to say. "It's more than that Kade. More than friendship."

I feel my eyes blink a few times, but it's out of my control. More than friendship? That couldn't possibly mean what I think it does, could it?

"You make me feel like I'm in control," she continues. "Like I can be myself completely. Like I can let my guard down with you and I'm not afraid that you'll hurt me."

"I would never."

"I know. And someday I hope I'll be able to feel that way about all our friends. I'm just not there yet." She looks up at me with an expression I've not seen from her before. It almost looks like… longing. "But I'm already there with you."

All my breath leaves my body. I've never been the guy girls fall for. Never even been the one they flirt with, except a few at the bar who want a drink on the house. But I'm almost positive Nicole is saying she likes me. *Likes* likes me. I don't understand how it's possible for a girl like her to want a guy like me but I want to know more. I have to know more. As much as I know she deserves someone so much better, I can't resist her pull and the way my heart wants to protect hers always.

All reasoning flies out the window, too engrossed in this moment and wanting to know more, to hear more, to feel more.

"What other things are you hopeful you'll be able to feel in the future?" My words are barely a whisper as I hold what little breath I have back, waiting for her answer.

Her eyes get glossy and she turns back to the television, as if she's ashamed of her answer. "I want to hold someone's hand without flinching."

I can't help it. I reach over slowly so as to not startle her and slide my hand under hers. I need her to know she can remove her clasp from mine whenever she chooses. That she's in control of this contact, no matter how innocent it may be.

Nicole looks down at our hands and a slow smile crosses her face as she intertwines our fingers. She never looks at me, just stares at the television, a look of contentment on her face as we sit side by side on the couch, just holding hands.

NINETEEN
Nicole

"**W**hat's wrong with you?" Paul asks as he moves around me to grab the bottle of liquor he needs.

For the first time in ages, he, Kiersten, and I are working together. That means Lauren and Annika are here for "girls' night" while poor Heath got stuck at home with my nephew. Not that he minds. I'm sure they're having some male bonding over building trains and chocolate milk.

"I just hate central Texas weather this time of year. It puts me in a bad mood."

It's unusually warm and sticky for November. I hate it. Inevitably it happens around the holidays every year, and it always irritates me. I want snow and cool temperatures to ring in the holiday season. Instead, the air conditioner is blowing a couple of weeks before Thanksgiving because the humidity is so bad, so I feel sticky even indoors.

Paul chuckles at my irrational mood. "I can crank the A/C down a little more so you can wear a sweater if that'll help."

"Maybe if you hire someone to bring in a truckload of snow. You know Carson would love that." I absentmindedly scoop ice into a couple of glasses while I think of all the things we could do with a truckload of flurries. "We could make snow angels and a snowman. Maybe have a snowball fight."

"And practically bankrupt me with the expense of it all…" Paul adds for good measure.

Pulling my shirt away from my body to try to find some cool air, the fantasy dies. "It wouldn't be so bad if the humidity wasn't so high right now."

He shrugs and places his drinks on a tray for Kiersten. "It'll be gone soon enough."

"Yeah, just in time for January and then I'll be in the Christmas spirit after it's all over," I grumble. He just laughs again. Glad he finds me so amusing these days. At least he isn't hovering as much anymore.

Well, that's not actually true. He just sends his friends to do the hovering now. Every time I work, at least one person he knows and trusts is here in bouncer mode. I could complain, but even I have to admit it allows me to breathe a bit easier.

"Watch this! Watch!" Lauren yells from her place at the bar, a few too many drinks in her already. One of the ESPN college stations is randomly rerunning her last National Championship gymnastics meet from a couple of years ago. It's making her even more excited than normal. She smacks Annika's arm a few times, a little too hard if the look on Annika's face is any indication. "This is Ellery's winning bar routine."

Kiersten drops her empty tray on the counter for Paul or I to put back. "Spoiler alert. What if I didn't know Ellery won that event?"

Lauren gives her a pointed look. "You were there live. If you missed it, you must have fallen asleep which makes you a bad friend. Come to think of it, all of you were there."

"I wasn't," Paul announces, getting in on the ribbing. "And now you ruined it."

Lauren rolls her eyes and her head lulls back. Annika immediately puts an arm behind her in case she falls off the stool. Surprisingly, she doesn't. She just quips back at Paul. "You're such a pain."

"Speaking of," I ask as I place the last couple of drinks Kiersten needs on the fresh tray. "Do you still keep in touch with Ellery?"

Lauren finishes a swig of her Apple Pie ale before answering me. "A little on social media but you know how it is. People grow apart. We weren't really great friends to begin with. More thrown together because of our mutual love of the sport."

I nod in understanding. "I get that. Some people are in your life for a reason…"

"And some for a season," she adds.

"And some last for a lifetime," Kiersten interjects. "Because you can't get rid of us."

Lauren and Annika clink glasses, although Annika's makes more of a *thunk* since it's a water bottle.

They go back to chatting and watching all the gymnastics they've already seen while the rest of us get back to work. I'm not sure if the weather is a factor, but it seems all the sports teams in the area had the same idea tonight and are here to cool off a bit.

The door opens and I groan as a wave of humidity hits me again. The feeling is short-lived though when the person who enters begins screaming.

"How could you? How could you do that to him?"

She's wearing a sweatshirt that's several sizes too big, and I vaguely recognize it from Jeremy's wardrobe. Her brown hair is pulled up into a messy bun and her face is swollen, like she's been crying.

And the screaming—it's directed at me.

Several patrons look our way, recognizing something is happening, especially when Kiersten races over. Before she can get in the middle of this though, I stop.

"Wait, Kiersten." I hold my hand up in front of her, halting her steps.

"What do you mean *wait*?" she hisses in my ear. "I'm not going to let Jeremy's new side piece come in here and throw a punch."

I can't take my eyes off the woman. Her distress is so intense, I realize how deep into the relationship she is. I can't help but wonder if she's more upset with me or with Jeremy. She can't take it out on him, though. That would put her in a dangerous position. Considering how humid it is outside, the giant sweatshirt makes me wonder what she's hiding underneath.

"She's not going to hit me," I say quietly to my sister, not wanting to draw any more attention to us.

"You don't know that."

"I do." I grab her hand and squeeze it. "She's hurting, not angry. Let me talk to her."

"You can't be serious—"

"I am. It'll be fine. Paul is here and so is Alex. If she so much as flinches, they'll intervene." I finally take my eyes off the woman to look at my sister imploringly. "She's his latest victim, Kiersten. She needs to know she's not alone."

Kiersten closes her eyes and purses her lips, but finally nods. "Fine. But I will call the cops if she so much as glares at you wrong."

"I know." Turning back to the woman, I approach slowly. I don't think she'll be spooked—she came looking for me after all. But I don't want her to think I'm here for a fight either. And I admit being a little nervous even if I know this is the right thing to do.

I stop a few paces away from her and keep my hands at my side. "Since you've tracked me down at work, I'm assuming you know who I am."

"Of course, I do," she spits out, eyes still wild with intense emotion. "You're Jeremy's ex-girlfriend Nicole and the cause of all of our problems."

That's not true and we both know it so I let the dig slide. "All I know about you is that you're his girlfriend. What's your name?"

"Faith." She sniffs and wipes her nose with the sleeve of the hoodie. She shifts back and forth like she has pent-up energy she's not sure what to do with. I suspect I know where the adrenaline comes from.

"I'm guessing he was arrested today?"

Faith's eyes snap up to mine and she glares at me. "Yes. But you knew that didn't you?"

I didn't, actually. The only time I talked to the DA, he said they were moving forward with pressing charges again. I'm still not entirely sure why they feel like a year-old domestic violence case is a priority but with an election coming up and a botched domestic violence case just a few months ago that led to some bad press, I suspect it has less to do with me and more to do with looking better to the public.

I shake my head in response to her question. "I knew it was coming at some point, but I didn't know when. That's not up to me."

Faith wipes her eyes and continues to fidget, seemingly

unaware of how many people are watching this exchange. "But you can stop it. You can make them drop the charges. You just have to say you were lying."

"I can't do that."

Kiersten pushes her way past me and flashes her phone in front of Faith's face. "Does this look like a lie?" From her wince, I can only assume there's a picture of me in the hospital on the screen.

"Kiersten, stop," I plead but she ignores me.

"He did that to her. And you want him to get away with it?"

I look over at Paul, hoping he'll intervene but he doesn't look all that upset by Kiersten's intrusion. Thankfully, Lauren is on it.

Slinging one arm over Kiersten's shoulder, Lauren tries to lead her away. "Come on K. Nicole's got this."

"No!" Kiersten practically screeches. "She needs to know what he did to her."

"I know," Lauren says gently and pulls her harder, remarkably sober all of the sudden. "Come here and cool off for a minute."

Kiersten mumbles something about hating that no one cares her baby sister was hurt so bad, but to her credit, she walks away.

I look again at Faith who has a fresh set of tears sliding down her cheeks as her fingers fidget together.

"Listen, Faith, I know this is hard. And I'm sorry for that. You must really like him to be this upset."

"He's just…" Her eyebrows furrow as she tries to hold back her emotion. "He loves me. No one has ever loved me like he does. How could you take that away from me?"

I expect her words to hurt more than they do. It's almost shocking to realize for the very first time I'm truly over him. I have absolutely no emotion good or bad, I'm indifferent to Jeremy and the course of his life.

It feels strangely good to recognize I have no desire for revenge or to get back at him. My motivation is truly about protecting myself and maybe giving Faith an out. That's it. Nothing more and nothing less. The realization feels like a giant weight lifting off my shoulders.

But it doesn't take away the fact that Faith is right in the middle of it all. Her involvement and her pain are why I feel like I need to handle this moment with sensitivity.

"I didn't take it away from you. But, Faith," I sigh, hoping she really hears what I have to say. "At some point, he will ruin all your illusions. You just saw the picture my sister showed you. It was of my face wasn't it? When I was in the hospital? He did that to me with his fist."

Faith scoffs and wipes her eyes again. "There's no proof he did that."

I take a small step closer, lowering my voice so only she can hear me. "You know I used to wear long sleeves when it was hot out, too, so no one would see the bruises."

She looks at me quickly, then looks around, terror suddenly filling her eyes. "You don't know what you're talking about."

"Maybe not. But if he is hurting you, now is a good time to get away from him before you end up like I did." She doesn't respond so I take a chance and push a little bit more. "Faith, if you need a place to figure out how to get away, you can always come here."

Her body suddenly goes rigid and she takes two steps back. "I won't." Her eyes blaze with anger. "You've ruined everything. You get to live with that, do you hear me? I never want to see your whore face again."

She turns and stalks out the door. I take a moment to

breathe in, two, three, four… hold, two, three, four… out, two, three, four… hold, two, three, four.

"You okay?" Paul comes up behind me and puts his hands on my shoulders. Kiersten, on the other hand, is still scowling but grabs a tray and gets back to work.

I glance up at him and give him a weak smile. "Yeah. I'm good. Really good, I think. I mean there's more to come, but I don't know. She just needed to be treated with a little kindness. I guess I've come a long way, huh?"

He swivels me around into a hug and pulls me close, kissing the top of my head. "You did the right thing. I'm proud of you kid."

His words feel good, but what feels even better is the fact that I'm proud of me, too.

TWENTY
Kade

"Put it down slowly," Jaxon demands, completely unconcerned with the fact I have a face full of branches.

"I can't. I'm being poked in the eye with a pine needle, you dick."

"Quit your bitching. This was your brilliant idea, not mine."

He's got me there. I've never had a Christmas tree in my life, but for some reason, it seems important for me to make the apartment festive while Nicole is staying here. I'll never admit that to him, though.

"Give me just a second." I fight with the tree trunk to get it in the base of the stand and try to unwedge myself from underneath the sappy branches. Maybe this wasn't such a hot idea after all.

As soon as I'm clear, Jaxon pushes it upright with a grunt.

We both stand back to admire our work.

"You know it's crooked, right?"

"Don't care," I say and walk over to the couch to drop myself on it, exhausted from all the exercise. "As long as it doesn't fall over, I'm not fixing it."

He drops down next to me and grabs a controller off the couch. I take that as my cue to turn our game on. "You plan on decorating it or just leaving it there to rot."

"Undecided. I'm starting to regret the whole thing." I begin pressing buttons to get everything set up so we finally do something I'm good at. Decorating is apparently not it.

"Yeah, well, in your excitement to impress your woman, you jumped the gun and got the tree about a month early."

"What do you mean?" I ask without looking at him, too engrossed in what I'm doing.

"I mean it's the middle of November. That sucker is going to dry up and become a fire hazard before you can jingle your own bells."

"Are you serious? Why didn't you tell me when I bought it?"

"I was having too much fun watching you make a fool of yourself."

I turn my avatar around and shoot his in the face.

"That was uncalled for you asshole." I have the distinct impression he thinks it was worth it for him to rib me.

"Shut up and play the game."

He chuckles and we both sit back, getting comfortable as we fall into the mindless rhythm of bank robberies and middle of town duals. It's rare that Jaxon has a day off that he's not spending with Annika, so as much as I want to be angry at him for letting me spend all that money on a tree that has a shorter shelf life than I realized, I'm too busy enjoying his easy company.

Brother or not, he's become one of my best friends over the years. Which is why I don't usually punch him in the nuts when he starts asking me personal questions.

"Have you asked her out yet?"

Usually.

I ignore his question, not wanting to discuss the elephant he's suddenly brought into the room. But of course, he won't let it go.

"Don't ignore me, Kade."

I grunt in irritation, partly from the topic and partly from losing focus. "No, I haven't asked her out. And like I told you, I'm not going to."

"Why not?"

"I'm not right for her."

"Says who?"

"Says everyone? Says society? I don't know how to answer that question. I'm just not. Get that wild boar right there. See him?"

I direct him to where I'm looking and he takes him out. Looks like he found our fake dinner.

"So, because she's gorgeous and you're just a normal dude who plays video games on his downtime, you're not right for her?"

"You *do* get it." My fingers move rapidly over the keys as I check out the animal and make sure he's alone. Those shitheads have been known to come in packs before unexpectedly.

"No, I don't get it," he argues. To his credit though, he takes out a copperhead while he does. "Do you see who I'm married to? Annika is a sports trainer for a professional football team. She's smart as fuck and the most beautiful woman in the world. I was on the practice team because I was good at reading stats. I wasn't just not a starter, I was like fifth string."

"And your dad is a football legend with a zillion dollars and you're in medical school."

"My adoptive dad," he corrects. "I can't claim those genetics so don't make me out to be better than I am. That's not my point anyway. Nicole likes you."

"She does not."

"You're literally the only person who doesn't believe it."

Or he's making things up in his brain. All we've done is hold hands, and that was more about her progress of feeling comfortable with people than it was about me. None of what he's saying makes sense. "For argument's sake since you clearly can't let this go, why would she even like me? She's surrounded by some of the smartest, best looking, richest men in Texas."

"Don't underestimate yourself. You're kind and fun and loyal. You always have a kind word for people and you go with the flow."

"You sure she likes me? Cause it sounds like you're the one with the crush on me."

He reaches over and punches me in the shoulder. Hard.

"Ow. Unnecessarily asshole."

"Totally necessary. She sees all those things *and* the fact that you fight for the people you love. Every chick wants that."

I snort a laugh. He's fucking hilarious today. "Oh yeah. I fight really well. More like I'd get my ass kicked by that dude Jeremy."

"And you still stepped in front of him when he came in to confront her."

"What are you talking about?" I squint to see the screen, sure I saw a flash of someone who may be stalking us. I bet the sheriff is out again.

"I heard that he was staring her down and you got between them so he couldn't see her."

I glance over at him and furrow my brows. "That? So what?"

"So, you basically stepped in front of a raging bull to protect her. Don't get me wrong, you're right when you say he could squash you. But you did it anyway. And that's the point."

I can feel my cheeks flushing the more he talks. "You make it sound like it was some big thing. It was just a reflex."

"Right. But it was an important reflex. It was protective in nature versus leaving her to deal with it on her own. Is there someone chasing us?" he asks, changing topics briefly.

"I think the sheriff might be looking for us because of a bank robbery, but I can't find him."

We play in silence for a few minutes until Jaxon decides to continue beating this dead horse he won't leave alone.

"You know you did it with Matty, too."

"You're losing me again. Can we just play instead of having this conversation?"

"No." He tosses his controller to the side, leaving me to my own devices.

"You shit," I grumble, but he ignores me.

"Remember that shoulder injury you were getting onto him about for not telling anyone?"

My thumbs slip off the controller, startled by his words. "You know about that?"

"Yeah. Dad called me to say how impressed he was that you got on Matty's case. He finally had an MRI done.

Turns out he has a small tear in his rotator cuff."

"Oh shit. Is he going to be okay?"

"Yeah, it's like a day surgery or something."

I shake my head knowing how pissed off Matty probably is. "He's going to hate that."

"Yep. But he's also thanking his lucky stars right now that you pushed him to finally tell the trainer what was really going on."

"Why?"

"Because he's only going to miss a couple of games. If he'd waited and it got worse, he could have been out permanently."

"No way."

"That's what I'm saying, Kade. You're responsible for him taking care of himself. You're good like that. You may not be six-five and two-fifty but that doesn't mean you're not a protector by nature. And Nicole digs your brand of protection."

I give him a pointed look before glancing back to the screen and getting yet another glimpse of law enforcement. "Are you drinking tonight?"

"What, you think she's interested in some huge guy that lifts on a daily basis?"

"She should be," I mutter.

"Get real. She can't even come out from behind the bar when people are there. But you? She stays in an enclosed area with you for hours with no problem."

I'm not sure if it's an insult that I don't have enough muscles to intimidate anyone, or a compliment that Nicole doesn't think I'd ever use what little muscle I have to harm her. I stay quiet as his words start to sink in. Is it possible she really does like me? I've wondered before but I don't want to get my hopes up either. There's no coming back from her breaking my heart.

Jaxon shoves me to get my attention. "You're starting to see what I'm talking about aren't you?"

"I mean, just because she trusts me doesn't mean she likes me like that."

Jaxon scoffs and tosses the free controller at my head, making me duck. "She plays *Red Dead Redemption* with you. You think she does that shit for fun?"

"I…" Now that he mentions it, maybe? "I thought she was enjoying herself."

"I'm sure she is. Because it's not about the game. She's enjoying spending time with *you*."

I go quiet, trying to process everything he's saying. It was one thing to think I see a small flirtation, but for someone else to see it—that's an entirely different thing. And it doesn't change the fact that I'm not good enough for her.

"This is all good information. But I'm not sure what you want me to do with it."

"I want you to take some initiative and ask. Her. Out. On a date. Not to your couch for more gaming with my brother."

I worry my bottom lip, distracted from my game, before asking the question I really want to know. "You really think she'll say yes?"

"I would stake my life on it."

Suddenly the sheriff I've been getting glimpses of comes from out of nowhere and slaps handcuffs on me.

Not a good sign of things to come. Not at all.

TWENTY-ONE
Nicole

"I'll see you tomorrow."

I pull out of the tight hug Kiersten has me in and cross my arms against what is finally a chilly evening. Still humid, but tolerable with the temps in the mid-60s. It puts me in a much better mood.

"Okay. Be safe."

She turns away and I watch as Alex walks Kiersten to her car. Technically he's here for me, but I was adamant that with my case coming to a head, anyone who works here needs an extra set of eyes until we know Jeremy's mental state. My sister especially.

Alex waits until she's safely in her car and pulls out of the space before jogging back inside. I shut the door behind him and lock it. I feel terrible he has to wait here for another hour or so with nothing to do.

Lately, it was decided, and I decided to gratefully go along with it, that I would always have male accompaniment when I close, which is several nights a week. I wanted to argue that it wasn't necessary, but deep down I already knew being alone in a dark parking lot in the middle of the night is already pretty unsafe. Add Jeremy to the mix and it's downright stupid.

Unfortunately, Kade and Paul don't always work the same shifts I do. In those cases, we have a few volunteers like Alex who pitch in.

"I'm sorry you're stuck being my security detail tonight, Alex."

He pulls back and looks at me like I've lost my mind. "Are you kidding? Paul says my next night here is on him just for hanging out and making sure you're okay. That sounds like a bargain to me. I can *drink* when I want to."

I smile at his emphasis on the word. He's always so fun to be around. "Well, it's appreciated."

Alex leans in and lowers his voice. "Between you and me, I would have done it for free. Just don't tell Paul that," he tacks on quickly.

"How come?"

He shrugs. "Every man I know can tell stories about his mom or sister or neighbor or friend being disrespected the way you were. Some of us want that to change, so we're doing our part to facilitate that. Besides," he smirks. "There are worse things than hanging out with a couple of pretty ladies late at night."

"You're such a charmer," Tammy says with a grin as she walks by, stopping to pat his cheek. They have such a funny relationship. It's this weird flirtation that isn't serious, but they just enjoy making each other smile. If I didn't know Tammy was madly in love with her husband of however many decades, I'd wonder about her more than I do.

I drop back behind the bar to begin the process of closing things down, even though one person still remains. It was also decided that since I don't know Alex that well, I have a second set of eyes—a female friend.

"And how did you get stuck being my secondary baby-sitter?" I ask Annika who is still sitting at the bar, nearly empty water bottle in her hand.

It feels a bit like I'm a "kept" woman from the 1800's with so many escorts. Not that I would mind living in Sanditon and having Theo James escort me everywhere. But I'm still ready to be done with this whole situation for several reasons—this being the biggest one.

"Jaxon is at your place anyway so I'm going to ride over with you when you're done."

Her answer sounds like a load of crap but I can't pinpoint exactly why.

"You know it's not my place, right? It's Kade's."

"You're staying there for now," she says with a shrug. "Close enough."

I grab the spray bottle and begin moving bottles over so I can wipe all the sticky alcohol off the shelves, but I can't dismiss the feeling that there's something else happening here.

"There's more to this than you meeting up with your boyfriend, isn't there. What's really going on?"

She quirks her lips before dropping the bottle on the counter and crossing her arms in front of her. "Mostly I wanted to see how you're feeling about the trial."

I glance up, my movements stuttering. I'm used to everyone tiptoeing around me and anything to do with the trial. It's still several months off but I wasn't expecting her to just come right out and ask about it. I'm not even sure what the answer is, so I go into default mode.

"I'm fine." I give her a bright smile and begin scrubbing again.

Oddly, Annika looks almost disappointed by my reaction. Like she was hoping for more honesty.

"That's good. You're stronger than most. I know when I had to testify against the man who raped me, I was terrified."

This time my movements stop completely. "You… you did that?"

She just nods.

"When?"

"Which part? The rape or the trial?"

Her matter-of-factness is almost jarring. I would expect such a sensitive topic to be discussed in hushed whispers behind closed doors. At least that's how I still feel about my case and there was no rape involved. Still, I can't stop my own curiosity. Not just because of what happened to her but because of how she dealt with it.

"Either I guess."

She pressed her lips together, then licks them before she answers. "Well, it took about six months to find him so the trial was almost a year after the rape. And I was nineteen then. Your age, I guess."

"No wonder I didn't know anything about it. I was in middle school then."

"Well, Kiersten and I weren't as close either. We didn't become true friends until Carson was born and then when she moved back here, we just fell into a deeper relationship naturally. Regardless, the biggest thing I remember is how hard the trial was on me." She looks off into space as if the memories are flashing through her mind. "I just wanted to move on with my life at that point and I couldn't until the most public part was over."

Tossing the rag aside, I lean in, curious about how she copes. "Did people try to make it your fault? Like asking why you didn't do anything to stop it or whatever?"

"Oh yeah. My family and I stopped reading the news partly for that reason. We stayed far away from all of it. But remember, it was an overly sensationalized story too." She raises her hand and begins absentmindedly running her finger over her bottom lip. "I was dating Jaxon who is famous for his own reasons—namely being the son of a football legend. And since he's the one who found me and stopped the assault, it was easy to put two and two together on campus. Word got out quickly. My name was everywhere. It felt like everyone was out for blood. Saying things like I shouldn't have left with… the guy or I should have worn a longer dress. Discouraging is an understatement."

I'm shocked by this revelation. "That's terrible. Why wouldn't you leave with him? People leave with hookups here all the time after a night out. If he seemed nice how could you have known?"

"Oh honey no." She drops her hand to mine briefly before pulling away. "I didn't leave with him. He drugged me and played it off that I was his drunk girlfriend. They let him take me right back into the alley."

I gasp, my hand flying to my cover my mouth, appalled that no one realized what was happening. That's when I put together one of her quirks. "That's why you always drink bottled water."

She shakes the empty bottle at me. "I can open it myself and make sure it's always closed. I can't believe you never put that together."

"I guess I never really thought about it. It just seems so… normal to everyone."

"That's because it is normal to everyone. Almost everyone surrounding you with support right now are the same people who surrounded me back then. It's not the first time we've been prepared for a trial."

I think over the timelines for a second, something not making sense. "Wait, even Paul?"

"He was Jaxon's boss back then. He was there that night. I'm pretty sure he's the one who called 911."

My jaw drops making her smile at my disbelief.

"I know. Believe me, the randomness of it is nothing I haven't thought of before. At some point, we'll all stop coupling off I guess. But so far, it's worked out okay for most of us."

A blush creeps up my face as I think about who I could potentially pair up with and how he's just across the apartment every single night. My reaction doesn't go unnoticed by her.

"Ah. I see there is another potential coupling happen."

"I don't… He just… We're…" I stumble.

Thankfully, she puts her hand over mine to stop me. "Stop. Whatever it is isn't anyone else's business. Besides, there's a lot of stress on you right now. Everyone's all up in your business and part of you wishes they would leave you alone but when they do you get kind of freaked out that they're gone. Am I right?"

I nod again. She's exactly right. I'm also kind of stunned by how open she's being. I admire that something as significant as a rape doesn't seem to have any control over her. She's always here and she comes in on her own. She doesn't care where she sits even when the teams are here. I wish I could feel that secure. I want to know how she did it. How she does it. And if there's any hope for me to ever heal like that too.

"Does it ever get better?" I ask quietly. "I mean, I know it won't ever go away totally. But like… do you still jump at unexpected noises or, or hyperventilate when you walk across the parking lot alone?"

"Up until the trial I felt like I was falling apart. It was awful. And even during the trial, Heath and Lauren had to stay at the apartment with us because I couldn't calm down with just Jaxon there. But once the anticipation of what it would be like was over, part of that dissipated. It will always be part of me. It's part of my story. But that chapter is over for the most part."

"You think I'll get there?"

She leans in and smiles at me. "I know you will. And I also know it's okay to be feeling however you are while you wait to find out what happens from here."

"Well, last I heard they were looking at a plea deal so I'm not sure how I'm feeling."

She taps her fingers on the counter. "I'm sure your thoughts are kind of all over the place."

"I just don't understand why they wouldn't want him to go to jail, you know?" I raise my hands in exasperation. "Like, maybe if I'd promised to cooperate back then, it would be different or something. Did I mess it all up by waiting too long?"

"No." She shakes her head vehemently "You can't think that way. You needed time to be strong enough to go through this. You weren't ready before. You are now. And honestly, you said he doesn't have any type of criminal record, so I'm not all that surprised they're trying to cut a deal. It sucks, but our legal system doesn't care as much about the victims as they pretend."

"I hate that. It makes me feel…"

"Worthless?"

My shoulders sag now that Annika's nailed it. "Yeah. That's exactly it. Like I'm not worth getting justice. I hate it."

She nods in understanding. "It's okay to feel that way, as long as you remember it's not the truth. You *do* deserve justice. And we're going to be here the whole way helping you get it."

I glance down at the floor and realize there's not much more that needs to be said, but I need to get back to work. "Thanks, Annika."

"Any time. And I mean that," she reiterates. "Even if you just want to process your thoughts or need to ask questions about what trial could be like. Call me."

"I will. I'm gonna get back to work so we can get out of here."

She covers her mouth with her hands as she yawns. "Yeah. Good idea."

"Want another water while you wait?"

"Sure. Might wake me up just a bit."

I hand her a fresh bottle and toss the old one, then get back to my cleaning. I'm a lot faster at closing than I used to be and soon enough Tammy and I are balancing the till and divvying out tips. She leaves with a smile on her face that I'm not sure if it's from Alex escorting her to her car, or the money she left with. Knowing Tammy, it could go either way.

Satisfied we're done and starting to feel drained from the day, I walk to Frankie's favorite booth where Alex is laying down and tap him on the foot.

"Hey," I say quietly, but it's no use. He lifts his head and breathes in quickly like I woke him up. "Are you sure you don't want me to call you an Uber? You fell asleep in the booth."

"That's because it's the most comfortable booth any-where." He reaches his long arm up to the top of the booth and pulls himself up to a sitting position. "No wonder

Frankie's name is on it. He was right. Damn."

"I know. But that still doesn't mean you're awake enough to drive home. It's late and you have to drop us still."

"And I'm still doing that." His tone gives me no room to argue. "Let's go."

I grab my purse, flipping off lights as the three of us head to the front door. We make our way through the parking lot, the evening air humid but with a crisp quality to it that gives me hope things are finally cooling off. I've lived in Central Texas long enough to know the weather lies regularly though.

We pile into Alex's non-descript giant black SUV. I'm not sure why he needs something so big, until he climbs into the driver's seat. It's sitting back so far to accommodate his legs, suddenly it makes sense why half the team drives something similar. They don't fit in anything else.

The drive to my… er… Kade's apartment just takes a few minutes. The area is well lit but Alex takes his job seriously and won't take no for an answer when he says he's walking us to the door. He's such a great guy. If I wasn't so hung up on Kade, Alex would be just the type of guy I'd go for.

Quickly I use my key to let us in and once Alex has safely delivered us, he salutes Jaxon with two fingers and takes off.

"'Night Alex. And thank you!" I whisper shout as he bounces down the stairs.

I no more than turn around to find Jaxon and Annika are already out the door. Annika grabs me into a quick hug.

"I meant what I said. If you need me, just call. I've been there. You won't hear any judgment from me, no matter what."

"Thank you." As soon as I release her, they leave, hand in hand.

Shutting the door, I make sure it's locked up tight. I'm really tired and don't want to come back out here to triple-check.

As I turn around, movement catches my attention. I startle before my brain realizes it's just Kade standing up slowly from the couch.

"Oh, Kade." My hand covers my heart. "Sorry. I didn't realize you were still up. I expected to see you dozing on the couch or something."

"Will you go out with me?"

His words are so unexpected, the meaning of them doesn't seem to translate.

"What?"

"I'm asking you on a date while it's late and I'm half asleep because it makes me brave and I'm terrified to ask you, so I'm doing it now. Do you want to go on a date with me?"

I can't help it. My lips begin to quirk up as the words finally sink in. He's nervous that I'll say no. It's so endearing, there's no way I can reject him.

"Yes. I'd love to go on a date with you."

He opens his mouth but then he stops to regroup. "Really?"

"Of course, I would."

He looks so perplexed it makes me want to laugh. "Huh. I did not see that coming."

"That I'd say yes?"

"Yeah, I kind of just assumed you'd say no and give me that whole 'we're friends' speech."

"Well, we are…"

"I knew it."

I take a quick step forward, trying to take back what he thinks he heard. "But that doesn't mean I don't want to see if there's more than friendship there, too. I like you Kade."

"You do?"

"I do. So yes. I'll go on a date with you." He continues to look baffled and I realize we need to end this conversation quickly. At this point, he might come to the conclusion he dreamed it. "You're right though. It is late and we're both half asleep at this point, so I'm going to get ready for bed. We can talk more about it in the morning okay?"

"Okay." He glances around like he's not sure what else to say. So, I put him out of his misery.

"Sleep well, Kade."

"You too, Nicole."

I make a pit stop in the bedroom to start my nighttime routine, and shut the door, leaning against it with a smile on my face. Just a few seconds later I have to put my ear to the door to see if I'm actually hearing what I think it is. Sure enough, it's the unmistaken noises of a guy doing some sort of happy dance moves floating through the door.

TWENTY-TWO

Kade

No one would ever mistake me for being a romantic kinda guy. I'm allergic to half a dozen different kinds of flowers, I don't know the first thing about flirting, and I broke out into a sweat trying to decide what to do on this date. After a week of mulling it over with not a lot of distraction since it was Thanksgiving week and people all but disappeared, my anxiety was so high I was going through deodorant like an athlete. So, I did the unthinkable—I asked Tammy for advice.

There is a possibility she and I have totally different ideas of what the word "date" means. She immediately recommended a book on kama sutra and a good lube. Her words, not mine. It was not the most comfortable conversation, that's for sure. But she did say one thing that stuck with me.

Go simple.

Of everything she said—most of it I suppressed to save my own mental health—that one made the most sense. By her logic, a date is about spending time with someone. Getting to know them on a deeper level. The more I thought about it, the more I realized all Nicole and I need to do is get away from our normal, everyday lives and distractions to just talk.

Today seemed like a great day to be outside with highs in the mid-60s. Now, we're trudging up this small hill, her carrying a large blanket and me carrying a couple of large bags.

"This would look so much better if I'd had a picnic basket."

Nicole laughs, her long blonde hair blowing gently in the breeze. "I don't know anyone who has a picnic basket. Besides, can you imagine how heavy one of those things would have to be to carry everything we need? I'd rather the bags. At least you can throw them away when we're done with them."

"You do have a point. And at least the weight is balanced equally on both sides."

We get to the top and Nicole points out a spot underneath the giant oak tree. "What about there?"

"Works for me."

We spread the blanket out and begin unpacking all the food from the bags.

"I wasn't sure what to bring so I brought a little of everything," I admit.

Nicole pulls out a container and opens it, eyes lighting up when she sees the cheese cubes. "Cheese, olives, crackers, salami—I feel like it's a make-shift charcuterie board. Just in plastic containers instead of on one of those wooden boards."

"That's what I was going for. I wasn't sure what to bring so I searched for some ideas online and this seemed like a good one."

"It's perfect." She pops an olive in her mouth and takes a deep breath in through her nose, a look of total contentment on her face. "The view from here is so pretty."

My cheeks flush at her compliment. "That's why I picked this hill. It's got the best scenery of anywhere on campus."

"And you've seen all the places?" she jokes and pulls a large bottle out of the bag. Her nose crinkles as she asks, "White wine?"

"Sparkling grape juice, actually."

Her lips quirk up in amusement. "Really?"

I shrug my response. "With as much time as we spend at the bar, I'm not all that interested in alcohol. But I figured it would be nice for the ambiance." I pull out two wine glasses I bought specifically because they seemed fancy enough for a picnic but not over the top. Handing them to her, I take the bottle and begin twisting the top open. Yes, it's a twist top. I didn't want to accidentally shoot myself in the eye with a cork.

"Have you decided if you're going to take that night class?" I ask, remembering the last conversation we had close to here.

"I don't know if I can," she says as she pulls out another plastic container, this one filled with chocolate sauce for dipping fruit.

"Why not?"

She looks at me like it's obvious, but I can see the disappointment behind her eyes. "I can't take three weeks off of work to take chemistry just to see if I can hack it in college again."

"Why not?"

She picks up the glasses and holds them out so I can pour the liquid in each one. It really does look like a sparkling wine. "I just started working and Paul needs the help. The class starts in three days. I can't just leave him in a lurch like that."

Closing the bottle, I balance it on the ground next to us, hoping it doesn't fall over. "Okay, I can see your hesitation. But maybe instead of assuming it's not doable, you need to ask him about it first. Wasn't Paul just saying the other day that the weeks between Thanksgiving and Christmas are pretty slow?"

"Well, yeah."

"If he can swing it with the schedule and it's what you want to do, why not?"

She grabs a slice of salami and pops it in her mouth, taking her time to eat it before continuing the discussion. "I also kind of need the money."

This is news to me. "Why?"

She looks me dead in the eye and says, "I need to start paying you rent."

Ah. So that's her issue. She feels like a freeloader.

"No, you don't."

"Kade." She smacks my leg gently. "I'm putting my foot down on that. I've been there for almost a month now. It's time for me to be a better roommate. It was one thing when I was crashing at your place. But I've basically moved in."

I shrug shyly, my cheeks flaming again. "I like that you've moved in."

Nicole's eyes widen just slightly before she bites her bottom lip. "You do?"

I nod, feeling uncomfortable telling her these things that feel so intimate, but wanting so badly to be confident that she feels the same way about me. Here goes nothing.

"I like having you around. I like hearing you laugh

when you talk to Carson on Facetime. And I like all your girly shit in the bathroom. I like seeing you come out of the bedroom first thing in the morning with your hair all messy and sticking up. I don't… want you to leave."

She takes a sip of her drink and makes a noise of satisfaction. "I don't really want to leave either, but you're making it sound like we're *living together* living together. This is our first date. Everything else sounds so… fast."

If only she knew how fast I would love to take this, even though I know she deserves so much better. Still, if Jaxon is right about her feelings for me, I have to at least try. A heartbreak, in the end, is worth getting to spend a little more time with her.

"I'm not asking you to move into my bedroom," I clarify as I open the last couple of containers of mixed vegetables and dip out, setting them on the blanket. "We can stay just friends at the apartment. We don't have to kiss or hold hands or anything you don't want. I just… I just want you to stay."

Nicole's hand reaches for my knee where it stays while she looks up at me, big blue eyes drawing me in. "I want to stay too. As long as you'll let me. And as long as you'll let me contribute to rent."

I could argue with her, but I won't. If paying rent is a deal-breaker, I'll just use her money on getting her favorite foods and chocolates anyway.

I've never felt myself smile bigger. As we look at each other, her hand still on my leg, the vibe begins to change. I take a chance and move closer. I won't do more than that, though. Not without her permission.

I force myself to gulp back the lump I suddenly have in my throat. "Is it, um… is it okay if I try to kiss you?"

She cocks her head and furrows her brows. "Try?"

"I don't know if I'm any good at it."

"Have you not done this before?"

The extent of my making out is limited to a game of Seven Minutes in Heaven and a girl named Carol Watson. It was neither seven minutes, nor heaven as Carol bitched almost the whole time about getting stuck in the closet with me. I don't want Nicole to think I'm a total loser though, so I lie. "Not very often."

The resulting smile is not at all what I expected from her. Nor is her response. "Good."

Taking the reins, she leans in and kisses me. It all takes me by surprise, her initiative, the softness of her lips, the way it sounds as we move our mouths together. I slide my hand behind her neck and she sighs softly into my mouth.

When our tongues finally touch, I about come undone with emotion. I have loved this woman for so long, my heart feels like it's beating for the first time.

Her hand comes up to my cheek, gently cupping my jaw as we continue to kiss. I never want this to end. I'm so grateful we're in public because I realize quickly I don't have very much self-control when it comes to anything sex related. Even something as innocent as a little tongue kissing.

As if she can sense my hesitation, Nicole pulls back and looks into my eyes. "Are you sure you aren't very experienced?"

That's not at all what I expected her to say. "Was it okay?"

"You kiss like a seasoned pro." I feel like a million bucks, especially as she leans in for more. "Let's do that again."

So, we do. I hear nothing, see nothing, feel nothing except her gentle breath on my lips and her soft tongue on mine. I can't make out many thoughts, fully in the moment. All I know is she's content, she's making happy sounds as I kiss her, and I may have convinced her to go back to school.

For the first time in my life, I'm finally doing something right.

TWENTY-THREE
Nicole

K ade was right.

I should never have assumed Paul would frown on me taking a night class. I was actually surprised at how easy it was to convince him I needed to take three weeks off.

At first, he hemmed and hawed because who wants their employee to take so much time off? But as soon as he found out what it was for, Paul practically dragged me down here to help me register. I keep checking to make sure he isn't having regrets, but Paul continues to be insistent that I need to take this step and it won't inconvenience him or the bar at all.

It helps that the protection order came in within days of Jeremy being arrested. Now he can't get within one hundred yards of me. Not that I expect him to try anything in public. That would be really stupid of him when he's waiting to go to trial. Or at least that's what I keep telling myself.

So, after all that concern and even more coordination,

here I am… officially a college student once again.

Walking into my first class since I dropped out, I can't help but smile. It feels good to be back, to be working toward my goals again, even if I'm not sure what they are anymore. I can't even be mad I'm taking a chemistry class. Sure, I was hoping to ease my way back in with something more my speed like beginning art, but the options were pretty limited.

With that thought in mind, I refuse to focus on the fact that I hate chemistry. While it's going to suck to be here for four hours every night, if I can knock it out in three weeks, it'll be worth it. That alone is something to be happy about.

Looking around the room, I try to decide where to sit. There is a dozen or so lab tables to choose from, each with two chairs. I assume that means whoever I sit next to will be my lab partner for the duration of the course.

Most of the tables are full and of the ones that have a seat open, the other is occupied by a guy. It shouldn't make me afraid. We're in a classroom with other people for goodness sake, but it does. I can feel my anxiety increasing, worrying my lip so much I'm sure all my lipstick is gone. Finally, I spot one seat open next to another woman. The relief I feel is palpable as I walk in her direction. Until recognition hits me.

She's the woman I saw at the store, Faith.

The same woman who confronted me at the bar.

She's Jeremy's new girlfriend.

From the way her eyes narrow and her lips purse, it's obvious she recognizes me too.

As uncomfortable as I may feel, though, I don't think she's a threat to my safety, so I continue on. Sitting gingerly, I place my backpack on the floor and pull my laptop out in preparation for class to begin.

One of her hands smacks down on the table as she huffs furiously. "Do you really have to sit here?" The venom in her voice is palpable. I do my best to ignore it.

"There aren't many other choices."

She looks around and gestures with her hand. "I see at least three other empty chairs."

Deciding I don't want to spend the next three weeks fighting with her, I try to level with her instead and address the topic both of us would probably rather avoid.

"I'm still nervous around men, okay?" I say quietly so no one will overhear. This is our business, no one else's. "I know you blame me for Jeremy being arrested but you being angry with me is still better than wondering if the guy I'm sitting next to is dangerous and will hurt me. As much as this isn't my preference any more than it is yours, can you at least pretend I'm not here so we can make it through the next three weeks?"

She blinks a few times, probably not expecting me to share something as vulnerable as my lingering fear of men. And if I'm right about her own relationship with Jeremy, part of her probably understands my plight as well.

"Fine," she concedes. "But I don't want to talk to you or become buddies or anything."

"Fine," I reply curtly. "Your name is Faith, right? Just in case I need it?"

"Yes," she says without looking at me.

"I'm Nicole."

"Oh, I know."

Maybe it would be safer sitting next to some random guy. If she's always this hostile, who knows what she'll do when she has access to various chemicals.

Fortunately, the professor comes in before I can think too much about that or for any more forced conversation to occur.

"I'm Professor Draman," he drones, just like I antici-pated a chemistry teacher would. "You can find the course's syllabus on my google classroom page." He points to his email address written on the whiteboard behind him. "I have paper copies for you as well. Please take one and pass the stack to the person behind you."

The papers are passed out to everyone and we spend the first two hours going over the syllabus of the class and hearing a basic lecture, before getting a small break to stretch our legs and use the facilities.

"Okay, class, go ahead and put your laptops away," Professor Draman announces when we reconvene. "We're going to do our first lab before you all head out for the night. It'll only take as long as you make it, so stay fo-cused. Everyone put these on."

People continue chitchatting as they follow the instruc-tions and put on the safety goggles the professor hands out.

We do a quick tour of the lab equipment and go over the rules, complete with a legal document we have to sign stating we understand it all and will do our best not to blow up the lab.

Well, it doesn't say those words exactly, but the guys behind us seem to find the comparison hilarious.

"Tonight's lab is going to be shorter and will help you become familiar with several instruments and how to use them. You have one set of the worksheets in front of you with all the instructions. The person you are next to will be your partner for the next three weeks, so make sure you work together. I want that one packet returned to me with both your names on it."

"Great," Faith mutters loud enough to make sure I hear her.

"Do you want me to start reading this out loud?" I ask kindly, refusing to lower myself to her level. I'm not the bad guy, no matter what she chooses to believe.

She shrugs with indifference at my question, so I begin.

"The accuracy of every measurement that is made depends on the equipment used to make the measurement," I read. "We will take mass measurements on a multiple beam balance and an analytical balance."

I remember doing a lab similar to this one in high school so we decide it's best for me to set up the various equipment while she writes everything down. It doesn't take us long to get going and find the information we need.

"Looks like it's 78.5 degrees Fahrenheit," I say and show her what I'm looking at for confirmation.

Faith looks at what I'm seeing and nods in agreement before writing down the answer. "What about Celsius?"

I look again, squinting because the numbers are really small. "11 degrees."

Again, she double-checks before writing it down.

"Next, we're doing length using two different metric rulers," she reads this time, her tone much calmer than it has been now that we're all business.

I move the thermometers out of the way and sort through our equipment for the rulers.

"You know he's out of jail, right?"

Or at least I thought we were all business. I don't know if she's trying to throw me off or if she just needs someone to talk to, but I almost drop the ruler when she drops that bomb on me. Partly because my heart stutters with my immediate fear reaction, but maybe more so because she shared at all.

"I know," I practically whisper, not wanting to say

something that will make her clam up again. I have this intense need to understand why Faith feels the need to bring it up. Just a couple of hours ago, she made sure we would never talk about him. So why did she change her mind? Why now?

"I thought you didn't want anything to do with him." Faith scratches at her sleeve and I want to ask if she has marks on her arm, but I refrain from asking.

"I don't."

"So why are you keeping tabs on him?"

"I'm not." I place the ruler where it needs to go and try to keep my eyes trained on the numbers I can't really see, so engrossed in where this conversation is going. "I was granted a protection order against him so I got a phone call that he made bail until the trial."

"Protection order?"

The obvious surprise in her voice has me looking over. I'm shocked to realize Jeremy didn't tell her anything about it. Then again, if he's still maintaining he's innocent, why would he? As long as he doesn't violate the order, she'd never have to know that the justice system doesn't trust him any more than I do.

There are so many things I want to say to her now that this information has come out. So many warnings I want to give her. But I feel so ill-prepared to even be having this conversation coupled with being afraid to give her any more details. It's not that I think she's dangerous to me, but what if she confronts him? Will he hurt her? Will he take out the rage on her that he has for me because I pushed this case through?

All the words I want to say are frozen on the tip of my tongue as my concerns race through my brain. I try to sort out the best course of action for this conversation but before I can come to any reasonable conclusions she sniffs and turns back to the paper.

"He never told me about that."

I don't respond. What is there to say? Despite her attempt at indifference, we both know this is the moment she's beginning to question everything Jeremy has told her, even if only one of us will admit it.

TWENTY-FOUR
Kade

My finger taps on the steering wheel to the beat of Kings of Leon's *Dancing in Your Head*. If they only knew all the feelings that have been dancing in my head for the last couple of months, they could write an entirely new song about it. Hell, I could probably write a song about it. It would be terrible and a worst seller, but at least it would get some of this out so I could sort through it.

This thing with Nicole is such a juxtaposition. On the one hand, I know I can't give her what she needs. I'm just a fledgling college student with no real path in life. Where I'm at now may very well be where I'm at in ten years. She deserves not just a man who has a plan, but who has the drive to get there. I'm not sure that will ever be me. Plus, I've seen my mother chasing that plan for my entire life and I have no interest in becoming like her.

On the flip side, I love Nicole. It took me a bit to wrap my brain around how big that feels, but it's true. Hell, when she kissed me, I wanted to bow down in front of her and beg her to keep me forever. Pathetic, I know. But she's everything I never dreamed I'd have in my life and in some ways, it's hard to contain my excitement at how things are turning out. I feel a little like a protective boyfriend, even though we haven't talked about the exclusivity of our relationship.

I'm still not sure if the depths of her feelings for me are as intense as mine for her. And I'm almost positive this is going to eventually end with my own devastation. But until that happens, I want to be with her as much as I can.

So here I sit, in my car in the parking lot in front of the science building at Southeastern State, my fingers drumming while I wait in the car for Nicole to get done. I was off work tonight anyway, so I offered to pick her up. If nothing else, I know it'll make her feel more secure that she won't be alone on campus at night.

People begin to trickle out of the science building and I step out of my car to walk over and greet her. Shoving my hands in my hoodie pocket to get a little more warmth, I stroll to the oversized concrete steps and lean against the brick wall.

Soon enough, I pick her out of the crowd just as she flips her long blonde hair over her shoulder. When she sees me, she smiles, but it doesn't reach her eyes.

That's weird. Was she not expecting me? Did I do something wrong? I can't quite gauge what's going on, even as she reaches me and tucks her arm into mine.

"What's the matter?" I ask, watching her face as we walk back toward the car, trying to get any indication of what's happening in her head.

"Let's just go," she says softly. The urgency in her tone has me immediately moving quicker. The tight way she's clinging to my arm has my hackles rising.

"Nicole, what is going on?" I ask again, afraid of her answer. The quickness in her steps and tension in her body has me on high alert.

"Nothing. Let's go."

As we make our way to the parking lot, I look up to make sure we're heading in the direction of my car and that's when I see him.

He's leaning against a giant black truck in the back of the parking lot, arms and legs crossed, a smirk on his face, and evil in his gaze.

"What the fuck."

Suddenly Nicole's insistence to get to the safety of my car makes more sense. How did she know he would be here? And I know this small side lot isn't one hundred yards long so why isn't she calling the cops right now?

"His girlfriend is in my class," she says quietly, and I notice she's refusing to look at him. "He's picking her up. We need to go."

I try to meet his murderous stare with one of my own but I'm sure it falls flat. I'd lose a fight with him in a matter of seconds and we both know it. The only protection we have from this psycho is a flimsy piece of paper that won't do anything to protect the woman I love from harm if this dick has his mind set on hurting her.

I hate that.

I usher her into the car quickly, making sure to lock the door as soon as she's inside, unlock it to climb into the driver's side, and relock it just as quickly. I don't even bother with a seatbelt, peeling out of the parking lot and onto the street, determined to get us away from him and to the safety of my apartment as quickly as possible.

"Slow down, Kade," Nicole pleads, and I finally notice how fast I'm driving. I immediately remove my foot from the gas pedal.

"Sorry."

"It's okay. I know you're mad."

I shake my head at how easily she can downplay this. "Mad doesn't even describe it. How dare that guy show up outside your class? Who does that?"

"A guy who is waiting for his new girlfriend."

Her answer is calm and matter of fact… and it confuses me. "Are you… defending him?"

"No."

"Because it kind of sounds like you're giving him a pass on this."

She leans back against the headrest and looks out the window. "It's not a pass really."

"Then what is it? Because I'm not understanding why you aren't more upset about this."

"I'm upset, but I don't think he knew I was going to be there. I think he was probably as surprised as we were."

"He didn't look surprised. He looked thrilled to mess with you again."

My fingers tap against the steering wheel but not to any beat. It's residual effects from the adrenaline racing through my body. My mind is spinning as I sort through what the next plan of action should be.

"I'm sure he was mad," Nicole continues, a little more nonchalant than I know what to do with. "He knows better than to come anywhere near me and technically he just violated the order. I could have him arrested."

"So why don't you?"

It's the million-dollar question I've been waiting the last few minutes to ask.

"Because of Faith."

She's lost me now. "Who?"

"Remember the girl who came in and yelled at me at work? His new girlfriend?"

"Yeah."

"Like I said, she's in my class."

I fight to keep control of the car, so shocked by this information I somehow missed the first time she said it. Now that it's sunk in, I can't help my flair of emotion. "What!?"

"We were both surprised to see each other."

"Why didn't you call me? I would have come to get you." I'm practically yelling now that I have this new information. "She didn't threaten you, did she? Because we can go back and ask them to add her to that protection order if we need to."

Nicole puts her hand on my arm trying to calm me down a bit.

"Kade. It's okay. She's harmless. She's my lab partner so I got to know her a little bit."

I groan in frustration at her lack of concern over her own safety. "Nicole…"

"No really, Kade. She's a victim like I was. She just doesn't want to admit it to herself yet."

My heart sinks as I finally realize what the real issue is. "Please don't tell me you're trying to help her get out of a dangerous relationship. You don't need to put yourself in harm's way like that. Not while he's still around."

"No, I…" she sighs again before restarting. "You can't help someone get out of an abusive relationship if they don't want out. I know that. It doesn't work that way. Ask Kiersten. She tried to help me before I ended up in the hospital and I shut her down every time. Wouldn't talk to her for weeks." She looks out the window again, either avoiding my gaze or just remembering. I'm not sure which. "Just from the few conversations we've had, Faith isn't ready. She might not ever be and I can't make her. But tonight, when we all accidentally ended up at the same place, I can let go of my feelings and at least show some respect and consideration. For her sake."

I rub my forehead, feeling the beginnings of a headache coming on. "I don't understand how that helps her at all."

"And I don't know that it will," she admits. "But tonight, Faith and Jeremy are worried I'm going to call the cops. Tonight, Jeremy will be on his best behavior so Faith can vouch for the fact that he didn't know I would be there and he never approached me and got out of there as soon as they could. Tonight, he'll be prepared to defend himself from any wrongdoing. If I poke that bear, he'll go off on her. I know it because I've experienced it. I don't want to take that risk over something that can be explained away this easily and won't end up with him arrested anyway."

I shake my head and grit my teeth. I don't like that she makes sense, but I know she's right. We were in a public place on the first night of a class they didn't know anyone else was taking. He never approached us and we were in each other's vicinity for thirty seconds max. It's a flimsy violation at best.

Nicole reaches over and grabs my hand, interlacing our fingers and grounding me. I can let it go this time, but with one change.

"Just, would you please text me next time something like this happens so I can be better prepared? Or so I can have Frankie or Alex or someone who has a fighting chance against him to pick you up instead?"

She kisses my knuckles and it makes my stomach jolt. It's distracting me from the issue, but no one has ever done that before. I like the way it feels. "I would have given you a heads up but we're not allowed to have our phones in class at all. The professor says it's too dangerous to have the distraction in the chem lab."

"Can you at least let the professor know you have a protective order against an ex-boyfriend so you can use it in the case of an emergency?"

She smiles gently. "I can do that. It won't change anything though. Jeremy's not enrolled in the class so it's not like he'll be coming to the classroom."

I nod even though I'm not sure I agree with her assumptions. Not sure at all.

TWENTY-FIVE

Kade was more shaken up about Jeremy showing up at school than I realized. I even suggested we play some *Red Dead Redemption* when we got home, hoping it would get some of his pent-up aggression out. I thought it worked. Apparently, I was mistaken.

This morning I woke up to Paul banging on our door and demanding I go with them to Heath and Lauren's house for a meeting. I said nothing, instead just looking at Kade for confirmation that he's the one who called my brother-in-law. Kade just shrugged like I should have expected it.

In all honestly, he's right. I should have expected a rallying of the troops. After the last year of getting to know these people, none of it should be a surprise. They're a bunch of busybodies who are all in each other's business, but I wouldn't have them any other way.

So here I am, playing with Carson while the rest of them discuss the situation and decide the best way to proceed. I almost feel jealous of Jaxon who couldn't be here because of his clinics. Lucky man.

This could be a really simple conversation because I can already tell them the answer… continue the way we have been and give it a rest. But no one wants to hear it from me. I tried for about thirty seconds when we got here but it became clear my ideas were unwelcome, so I gave up temporarily. I'm giving them all a chance to let off some steam before I push back.

Besides, this really is an amazing train set. I have no idea where Heath found it, but it's a dining-room-sized table with all these tracks Carson can connect to make whatever design he wants. And the train runs on battery power so as soon as he's done building, the train will go on its own.

Whenever he's finally done, that is. He keeps building and rebuilding until he gets it just right. I suppose there are worse ways to pass the time while everyone else decides on my life plan.

"Not like that NicNic." Carson, also known as Spider-man since he still refuses to take off his Halloween costume a month later, takes the pieces out of my hand. "I'll do it."

"I thought that's how you wanted me to do it."

"No. It's wrong. I'll do it for you."

"Et tu, Carson? You don't believe I can get things done myself either?"

He looks at me blankly, probably because he doesn't speak Latin, then goes back to building, putting the pieces together the exact same way I did before he insisted it was wrong. Seems like the story of my life these days.

"She just needs to call the police and report it," I hear Paul say for the umpteenth time as he continues to pace on the large patio. He's been walking back and forth since we got here. I suspect he did that all last night as well. "That's just all there is to it."

"I'm not calling the cops," I announce for the umpteenth time myself.

Paul throws his hands in the air, obviously exasperated that I won't get on board with his ideas. "And why not?"

"I already told you why but no one likes my answer."

"That's because it's ludicrous."

Kiersten, who is wrapped up in a fuzzy blanket to ward off the chill of the day, puts her hand on his arm to calm him. "What he means is we heard you, we just don't understand."

I shrug. "That's because none of you have been in a relationship like that before. While I was in it, I couldn't really see some of his triggers but now that I have some distance, it's a lot clearer. And I'm not going to put someone else in harm's way for no reason. I don't want to be that person."

Paul takes a step forward to start ranting again, but Kiersten pulls him back. "Then why don't you give us some ideas on how to handle this situation."

I stand up and brush the dirt off my rear, pulling my hoodie up on my head and approaching the group now that they've finally asked for my input. "Like I keep saying, we keep doing what we're doing, which for the record, I still think is excessive…"

Paul tries to interrupt but I hold up my hand and continue. "… but with Jeremy around, I'll at least concede to being escorted everywhere for a while."

"Well, we're tightening up security," Paul demands. "And Kade can't escort you anymore. He can't defend you. He's too small."

I punch him on the arm, which causes no pain to him whatsoever, and shoot him a glare. "That was so rude

Paul."

"It's true though."

"It is not. But you sure are being a bully right now and I'm going to pull you off my security detail if you don't quit."

"No, he's right," Kade interjects, looking dejectedly at his hands as he leans on his elbows. "I can't protect you. You'd just end up getting hurt around me."

I rush over and sit next to him. "Kade don't listen to Paul. He's being overly cautious and ridiculous. Besides, if Jeremy wants to hurt me, he's not going to throw a punch in the middle of the street. That would be stupid. No one can stop him if he's really that determined."

"Frankie could," Paul grumbles making me whip my head up and glare at him again. I know Kade is having a hard enough time of it without Paul's continual reminders that my boyfriend isn't a professional athlete like the rest of them.

Or at least I think he's my boyfriend. We didn't get that far before everything hit the fan again.

"She's right, Paul." Heath fidgets with his glass of dark liquor, making the ice cubes clink together. "If he shows up with a gun, there's nothing any of us can do except pray the cops get there in time."

"That doesn't make me feel better," Paul growls, hands on his hips.

"It's not about making you feel better," Annika interjects. "It's about making Nicole feel better. She's the person we have to concentrate on." Annika turns to me. "What do you want to do?"

I smile gratefully at her. She's the first person to actually ask me that and demand that everyone else listen.

"Ideally, I'd love for this to all go away."

"I know." And she really does. Of that, I have no doubt. "But we have to be realistic, too."

"Look," I lean on my own elbows and look everyone in the eye, one by one. "I don't mind having someone drive me to and from school. I mean, I'd love to go on my own just because I'm tired of being afraid and I never seem to have any alone time anymore. But until he's sentenced, I know that Jeremy's a loose cannon, and being on my own isn't smart."

"I don't understand why he's even in town," Lauren says, stretching out her legs on the lounger she's sitting on. "Isn't he supposed to stay in the county he was arrested in or something?"

"From what I was told, he requested to come back here since he has a job or whatever." It wasn't the explanation I had wanted from the DA when I'd asked about it, but I understood that if a judge orders it, it doesn't matter what I want.

"Where is he working?" Heath asks.

"I don't know. I didn't ask."

"That would be good information to know." Paul's tone still sounds angry.

"With the way you keep pacing and are barely holding it together, I'd argue it's better you don't know."

He narrows his eyes at my retort, but I narrow them right back. I love Paul, but the man needs a Xanax or something.

"Do you really think that's going to be enough, though, Nicole?" Lauren's question diverts the conversation back to where it needs to be. "Right up to the trial was almost harder on Annika than any other time. Hell, Heath was sleeping on an air mattress in front of their bedroom door even with Jaxon in her bed so she could sleep at night."

"My back still hurts from that damn thing." Heath flashes Annika a quick wink so she knows he's kidding.

"I get what you're saying, Lauren but it's not the same thing," Annika replies. "I had no idea who had assaulted me. I never saw his face so it could have been anyone who walked by. That messed with my brain a lot. Nicole knows what Jeremy looks like. We all do. We know what the threat looks like and who we have our eyes open for.

"Plus, my attack happened when I was drugged so any dream-like state freaked me out. I was afraid to be unconscious at all and to wake up and find it had happened again. Nicole isn't battling that semi-conscious fear."

"Speaking of, did your nightmares finally go away?" Kiersten asks, sitting down across from me. For the first time, my mind feels more at ease—like they're all finally listening and including me in on the conversation.

"Not totally. But Annika's right. Her situation and mine are totally different. No one's experience of any kind of abuse is exactly the same and no one's reactions are identical either. You can't just decide what is going to be best for me without my input. It doesn't work that way."

"You're right," Kiersten says apologetically. "We just get really upset and want to do whatever it takes to protect you."

I grab her hand and squeeze. "And I love you for that. Even you Paul, despite the smoke coming out of your ears." He doesn't look amused at my comment but at least he's not pacing anymore. "Don't make it worse by not letting me have any freedom either. I'm finally feeling more like myself again. I don't want to lose that."

"I'm sorry. We both are, aren't we Paul?" Kiersten looks up at him, using her mom glare, one eyebrow higher than the other.

"Yeah. I'm sorry, too. And I'm sorry Kade," he offers. "I wasn't trying to be a dick. It's just… she's my sister."

"No apology necessary. I'd probably feel the same way about Lucy even though she's really Jaxon's sister." I smile at Kade and bump his shoulder, hoping to reassure him that none of the crap Paul has been spewing has made me question him for one second.

"So, it's settled then," Heath announces. "We'll continue to escort Nicole to and from school…"

"For now," I interrupt.

"For now," Heath adds with a nod of recognition my way. "And when she goes back to work, we'll do a rotation then as well."

"For the time being," I interject again. "Seriously, y'all. You can't do this forever. If Jeremy doesn't get any jail time, this could last for a really long time. There's no reason for that."

"We'll see on that part," Paul demands. "I can do this the rest of my life."

"No, you can't. You have a family."

"Which you are part of."

"Your child is going to need you sometimes, too. Paul." He finally looks at me. Really looks at me. "I love you. And I love that you consider me your sister. I've always wanted a big brother. But this isn't healthy. You have to stop."

He looks down at the ground, his lips firmly pressed together. "I hear ya."

"Do you?"

He nods, reluctant to recognize I'm right but setting aside his pride anyway. "Yeah. You are a strong, independent woman or some crap like that and I have to let you decide what's good for you."

"Exactly. Thank you."

Lauren claps her hands together. "Now that it's all sorted out, can we please fire up the grill? I'm starving." For as small as she is, that woman eats all the time.

"On it, my love." Heath jumps up and drops a kiss onto her lips as he walks by, probably as grateful to have finished this conversation as I am.

"I'm going to grab some water," Kade says to me and pats my knee before walking into the house.

"He's been awfully quiet," Annika whispers to me. "I know he's not a huge talker, but even for him, he's acting weird."

I noticed it too and my gut says something is wrong.

"I know. I'll be right back."

Everyone ignores me as I follow after him, too busy giving Heath their orders. I approach Kade in the kitchen. He's nowhere near the fridge or the water he said he was getting and the vibe I'm feeling isn't a good one. My heart rate picks up as a sense of foreboding takes over.

"Are you okay?"

He doesn't turn around instead, inhaling deeply before he answers.

"Yep."

I take a step forward, wanting to put my arms around him but somehow knowing that's not the right thing to do in this moment. "Is this about what Paul said? He's just being a jerk because he's overprotective. Ignore him like I do."

"No. He's right."

This isn't good. If he's siding with Paul's crazy rants, what will that mean for us?

"He is not," I argue, a sense of desperation beginning to take over. "You heard Heath. Nothing can stop Jeremy if he's really determined to hurt me."

"That doesn't make me feel better."

I've finally had enough of talking to his back so I step in front of him and lean down a bit to force him to make eye contact with me since he's still looking at the floor.

"Kade, nothing is going to happen to me. Not when you're around or even when you're not. But either way, I like it when you're with me." I take another step forward. "I like being with you. You make me happy and make me feel like everything is going to be okay."

I reach out to take his hand but he pulls back. "You need to move out."

I flinch back from the shock of his words. "What?"

"Yeah. You have to go. My um… my roommate decided to move in and he needs his room back."

I narrow my eyes at him. "You're lying to me."

"Nope. He texted me that he and his girlfriend broke up and since he's been paying his portion of the rent all this time so his parents didn't find out..." He waves his phone in my direction as if that's proof enough. It's not.

"Show me," I demand, not willing to play this stupid game with him. But God, if he's going to do something drastic like this, I want proof it's for a good reason and not because Paul has a tendency to get singularly focused and forget the damage his words can do if he's not thinking straight.

Kade doesn't bite, though. He throws his hands up in the air instead. "Dammit, Nicole. It doesn't matter if you believe me. It's my apartment. I'm telling you to move out."

I feel I've been punched in the gut as all the breath in my lungs leaves me. "But I… I don't want to move back into the bar apartment." And not just because I like living with him. The thought of going back there, of being alone there, makes my stomach hurt.

"I know." I swear there is a hint of sadness in his voice. "That's why you're going to move in with your sister."

"Kade," I plead taking another step forward but he backs up again.

"No." He squares his shoulders and I know he's not going to back down. It's over. Whatever we had, whatever relationship we were building is gone. "I need you to leave. I don't want you there. It's too much. Too hard on me. I need out."

I bite down on my lip, trying not to let the tears that have suddenly filled my eyes fall.

"I work tonight so that'll be a good time to come get your stuff." He glances up at me for a split second, his eyes dull with a complete lack of emotion. "I have to get to class. I'll see you later."

Kade turns and walks out the door, not looking back as he leaves me and my shattered heart in a giant mess in the kitchen.

TWENTY-SIX

Kade

The sound of Tammy's tray dropping on the counter makes me jump. I bite back a snarky comment, knowing my bad mood has nothing to do with her and everything to do with the pathetic state of my love life. For once I finally started to have one, only for it to get cut off by a raging maniac that can't leave the woman I love alone.

"What crawled up your patootie and died," Tammy asks, as if I'm going to share my heartache with her.

"Nothing."

"Now you've reverted to lying. You don't have to tell me, but don't pretend you're all sunshine and roses today either."

"I've never pretended that."

"Good thing. You have a terrible poker face."

She's goading me but I won't bite. I have no energy for it. I just want to do my job, go home, and mindlessly play some *Red Dead Renegade* in story mode so no one bothers me until I pass out from exhaustion. Conversation isn't part of that list.

"That's why I don't play cards. What do you need, Tammy? Another apple pie for Dwayne?"

"Nope. He's in full-on hustle mode today." She gestures over her shoulder with her thumb, I assume at the pool table. "He wants a water, please. But Liam asked for whatever IPA is on tap tonight."

"Liam's here?" Interesting. I haven't seen him in weeks. I wonder where he's been. Not enough to inquire, though.

"You really aren't paying attention, are you? He's been here for over an hour."

I shrug nonchalantly and grab a fresh mug for his drink. "I guess I thought they had an away game or something."

"They did." She leans in and lowers her voice as if she has insider information. Knowing her, she might. Not that I care right now. "He's been side-lined because of an injury. Hoping to get back on the road next week. Seriously, how do you work in a sports bar and not know these things?"

"You know this wasn't always a sports bar," I say as I put the IPA on her tray.

"Embrace the change, kid."

"Says the woman who refuses to use the new computer system to put in orders and payout tabs."

She scowls at me. "That's different. There ain't nothing wrong with talkin' to a person to place an order. This is why you kids don't have any social skills. You're always on your computers."

"I have social skills."

She cocks her head back and gives me a pointed look. "Is that what you call being in a huff all night? Your social skills?"

"That's called being in a bad mood. Not the same thing."

"Both ways make my life harder."

I place the bottle of water on her tray. "Don't you have some drinks to deliver?"

She picks it up and walks away grumbling about moody teenagers. Jokes on her. I'm in my twenties.

Turning back to the customers at the bar, I see Heath waiting patiently. I sigh knowing he's probably here to have another conversation I don't want to have. Best to get it over with so I can move on with my life.

I place my hands on the counter, prepping myself. "What can I get you, Heath?"

"An explanation."

"We don't serve that here."

Heath taps the counter and stares at me, but I don't look away. I'm not in the mood to discuss Nicole or Jeremy or what might have been the biggest mistake I've ever made. And I'm certainly not going to discuss it at work.

Finally, he caves and looks away first. "I can see you're going to be a tougher opponent than I gave you credit for." He tries for some humor but it falls flat on me. "Okay then. Do you know how to make that Sazerac thing Paul makes me?"

"Yup." I begin grabbing everything I need, thankful it's not a hard drink to make which means this conversation will hopefully be short-lived.

I'm sure the silence feels awkward on his end, but I'm too amped up to feel anything except frustration.

"You don't even want to know how she was after you left?"

And maybe a little bit of guilt for leaving things the way I did.

I keep my eyes on the sugar cubes I'm muddling but yield to him this time. "How was she?"

"A mess, man."

I add some ice cubes and the liquor, still refusing to look at him. "That wasn't my intent."

"I figured. But the question is, what was your intent? Because she won't say anything except you need the room back in your apartment…"

"That's right."

"… which we both know is bullshit."

Finally fed up, I slam my hands down on the counter. "What do you want from me? I can't protect her. There's a…a… a madman on the loose and there's nothing I can do."

"So, kicking her out was the way to go?"

"You heard Paul. I can't help her." I go back to my work, rolling some absinthe around in another chilled glass, more as a way to keep myself occupied than because I care if his thirst gets quenched right now. "The most used muscles on my whole body are my thumbs from playing video games. I'm not fast. I'm a little on the chunky side and would probably get knocked out with one punch. Where does that leave her, huh? Vulnerable. I can't put her in that position. No matter how much it hurts her or me I won't do that to her."

Heath rubs his cheek thoughtfully before responding at all. "You gonna finish making my drink or keep rolling that around while you spew more crap at me?"

I shake my head and begin straining all the liquid into the new glass so I can hurry up and hand it over to him, ready to walk away. Damn him for choosing a drink that has so many steps to it.

He takes a slow breath before speaking again. "It always baffles me when a man pushes the woman he loves aside because of his own pride."

I can't help the eye roll as I finally place the drink in front of him. "It's not about pride. It's about safety."

"Nope. Not buying it." He takes a slow sip of his drink while I clean up. It's not slow enough for me to finish and move on, unfortunately. "Nicole's right you know. If he has a gun, even Frankie can't stop him. No one can. And yet, she wants to be with you no matter what."

"That doesn't matter," I say through my teeth.

"Seems to me it should be the most important matter of it all."

I drop my head back, frustrated that I can't get him to understand. "Don't you get it? I'm not good enough for her. She needs someone who doesn't just protect her but can provide for her and take her to fancy dinners and give her gifts of jewelry. She's worth so much more than I am. She deserves so much better than me."

And I'm not the only one who knows it, I think to myself. I keep those words inside, though.

Heath stares at me thoughtfully. "Sounds like you're less worried about protecting her and more worried about not deserving her."

"What?" I put the liquor away with a little more force than I probably should. "That's not what I said."

His chuckle is low and slow. I don't like it. Makes me feel like he's got some sort of ace up his sleeve I'm not going to enjoy finding out about.

"We've all done it. Me, Jaxon, even Paul. Pushed away the woman we loved because of some random excuse that's really a way to protect ourselves from getting hurt."

Now he's just getting on my nerves.

"You don't think it hurt to make her move out? I hate going home to an empty apartment. But it's not about me. It's about what she needs. The end."

"You forget I'm Jaxon's best friend. I was there when you showed up on our dorm room doorstep all those years ago and I was in the room when the DNA test came back." Shit. I knew I wasn't going to like this. "I know you were raised without anyone paying attention to you and that jacked with your head. But Kade, that doesn't have anything to do with you. That has everything to do with them. Even your mother." He holds his hands up defensively when he sees I want to respond. "I don't mean any disrespect by saying that but I know how distant she is and that's her issue. The way I see it, she's the one who missed out on your life, not vice versa. But Nicole *sees* you and wants you exactly the way you are. You really want to push her away like that?"

"She wants me now. When she's afraid and doesn't want to be alone. That's why it's better for her to be with her sister. She'll start to realize I was just filling a void for her."

It hurts to say those words out loud, but it's the truth. Better that I figure that out now than a year from now. A heart can only break as badly as it's been used, right?

Heath quickly drains his glass and places it on the counter, ready to retort, but Frankie approaches and claps him on the back first.

"What are you doing at the bar, man? We gettin' a table?" Frankie asks with a smile. It's no wonder he's happy. This is the first time I've seen him here for some fun instead of to provide protection in a while.

Heath fist bumps his teammate and gestures his head in greeting at Alex who is talking with someone else across the way. "Yeah. I'm just chatting with Kade while I wait for you losers who could have been here on time if you didn't have your head up your ass."

Frankie smooths down his shirt and looks around the room. "At least we made it. I'm grabbing my booth before someone takes it."

"I'll meet you over there in a second."

"Cool. What's up, Kade?" Frankie says quickly and then jogs over to his favorite table. His overwhelming preference for that one spot would be humorous if I wasn't in such a bad mood. Still, I feel like maybe I've been too hard on Heath since he walked in and maybe I need to address it.

"So, you didn't just come here to lecture me?"

"Nah. I already had plans with the guys. Can't blame me for tracking you down while I'm here though." He pushes up from the stool to join his friends. "Think about what I said. Nicole is the sweetest and you're never going to get another chance with a woman like her. Don't let some deep-seated mommy issues scare you away from the best thing that ever happened to you."

With that he joins his buddies for a night of camaraderie while I'm behind the bar, replaying his words over and over in my head.

TWENTY-SEVEN
Nicole

"What time do you have to leave for class?" Kiersten asks as she plops down next to me on the fancy new sofa Paul got her a few weeks ago. It's a dark shade of green and soft enough that I want to take a nap on it one of these days. That is if I could get Carson to move over and not stay suctioned to me while he watches Paw Patrol.

"About five-thirty."

"Do you know who is driving you?"

I shake my head and swallow the lump in my throat. It should be Kade taking me to class today but now that he's done with me I neither know nor care who will take his place. Someone else can decide. "I'm sure Paul will let me know at some point."

"Nic, you know Paul didn't mean those things he said, right? He's just really scared for you." She puts her arm around my shoulder and tries to tug me close, which is almost impossible to do with Carson clinging to me on the other side.

"I know that." My words come out more like a whisper.

"I don't think you do. I think… how do I explain this." She goes quiet for a few seconds, likely trying to find words she can use with little ears sitting so close. "I think being there when Jaxon found Annika after she was attacked has stayed with Paul more than he even admits sometimes."

"You think?" I'd never thought about that. I was so into Annika's side of the story, I'd never stopped to think about Paul's.

Kiersten nods, recognizing my surprise. "Haven't you noticed the signs in the ladies' restroom?"

I think for a second. "Which ones? The ones that show us how to wash our hands the right way?"

"Ha! No. Although I'm always shocked that people don't already know how to clean their hands." I nod in agreement because seriously. It's like the number one thing they've been teaching Carson at daycare. He corrects us when we don't count to twenty regularly. "No, I'm talking about the Angela signs."

Now I know what she's talking about. "The ones that say, 'If you feel you are in danger, come to the bar and ask for Angela. We'll help keep you safe.'"

"Those are them. I don't think Paul's ever forgiven himself for not having a system in place at the club he and Jax used to work at. Or maybe they did but they didn't have signs or something. I don't know. Anyway, that's why it's part of the new employee orientation. He's a little hypervigilant with safety. Especially when it comes to you." She shakes my shoulders slightly, trying to lighten up the situation. It doesn't work.

"That's understandable. Commendable even. Except none of it gives Paul the right to insult Kade the way he did. Did you see the look on Kade's face? Like he was…

worthless." My body deflates as I think about how beat-down Kade looked. I wanted to run over to him and tell him he's the best person I've ever known. That he's the most handsome, fun, loving, perfect person in my life, but I was afraid if I was as over the top as Paul, but in the opposite way, it would embarrass Kade even more. So, I kept my mouth shut. And now I have regrets.

"Paul knows that. And we had a long talk about it last night."

"You did?"

"We did. He plans on apologizing to Kade tonight. Maybe give him a raise or something. I don't know. For what it's worth, he feels really bad about the whole thing and doesn't want you and Kade to break up."

I scoff.

"Seriously," she continues. "Paul is always going to have a bit of a protective streak over you. When he finally got over his own insecurities, he decided to take this patriarch of the family thing to a whole different level. Combine that with the Annika issues and with the fact that the first time he met you, you had a broken wrist. It makes a perfect storm of emotion."

I grimace. I had forgotten the first time we met was right after I had gotten back from the hospital and my face still looked like I'd been in a massive car accident.

"But he likes Kade. And he likes Kade with you. Even if he gives you shit about it."

"That's a bad word, mama," Carson says absent-mindedly, still staring at the screen. I'll never understand how little kids can always pick out the one word or topic they shouldn't when they're so deeply engrossed in cartoons.

"You're right sweetie. Thanks for that," Kiersten says with a chuckle before addressing me again. "So, what are you going to do about Kade anyway?"

"What is there to do? He kicked me out. As much as I love him—"

Kiersten gasps. "You love him? That's so much more than I thought."

"Well yeah," I say like her reaction is the dumbest thing I've ever heard. "How could I not? He's just… amazing. No one has ever looked at me like he does. Like he'd give up his own happiness for me. Like nothing else in the world matters except…" I pause as it hits me. "… me and my well-being. Oh, Kiersten."

I look at my sister with tears in my eyes. "He didn't kick me out. He sacrificed his happiness for my well-being."

She smiles sympathetically. "It appears that he did. And I have to say, I didn't see that coming. Not one bit. I thought he was just being kind of a whiny brat, to be honest."

"Kiersten!" I reprimand with a laugh. "How can you say that?"

She tries to shrug but can't in this position, so she removes her arm from around my shoulder. "I guess I've dated a few too many people. Most of them are, in fact, whiny brats when their feelings get hurt. It was a reasonable assumption."

"Except it was the wrong one and now I really don't know what to do."

"Normally I'd say wait for him to come to his senses so you don't look desperate, but I don't think that's the right course of action this time."

"You don't?"

"No." She draws her knees to her chest and rests her cheek on her knee. "I think Kade is always going to try to sacrifice his own happiness for you. So, this may be a case of always making sure he knows how happy you are with him."

I bite my lip as the different options in front of me play out. "Maybe I should go over there and demand he listens when I tell him I love him."

"You are the one who said everyone has different reactions to bad situations."

She's right. I did. Only I was talking about Faith's reaction to abuse, not Kade's reaction to being emasculated in front of all our friends. Still, it's not like he grew up with stability and parents who reminded him regularly he was loved. So how would he know how deeply I feel for him if I never told him in those exact words?

I stare at the TV again as I think through his schedule and where he'll be right now. His classes should be over and the bar doesn't open for a few hours. He's probably at home playing *Red Dead Redemption*.

I think I know what I have to do, but it still makes me nervous. "Do you want to go with me to his apartment?"

Kiersten laughs lightly. "Oh, we're still not letting you out of our sight in public so of course I'm going."

I pat her on the leg, feeling a sudden burst of excitement. "Let me go get dressed first."

I head into Carson's room where I've been crashing, much to his delight. The three a.m. wake-up calls as he climbs in the twin bed with me isn't as much fun for me as it is for him. It might take a few minutes to get the bags under my eyes in control.

As I riffle through my suitcase to find something clean and decent to wear, I hear my phone. I don't recognize the number but I know that area code well and know better than to send it to voicemail.

Taking a deep breath, I swipe to answer. "Hello?"

"Hello is this Nicole Willoughby?"

"Yes." I sink down onto the small bed, my legs suddenly unable to hold me up anymore.

"My name is Reginald Thurston. I'm the Assistant District attorney in charge of your case against Jeremy Letterman. I wanted to update you real quick so you know what's happening."

I take a deep, centering breath. "Okay. I'm ready."

"It's finally over Ms. Willoughby. He's going to jail."

TWENTY-EIGHT
Kade

"Okay, guys. The trick to doing a proper push-up is to make sure your form is correct." The guy on my television is buff and tan and trying not to sound condescending, but I can't help wondering how much he can bench, which isn't good for my focus or my ego. I have a goal here. I need to stay on track.

I squint my eyes again, trying to see past the masculine blob to what he's doing and compare it to what position I'm in. Sadly, I can't really see his form without my glasses on, but I can't wear them to exercise without them falling off either, as I get sweaty. And I really don't want to get one of those bands to hold them on my head. This is humiliating enough.

"When you push up onto your toes, suck in your stomach, like you're trying to get your belly button to touch your spine."

I do what he says and suck in. I'm not sure my stomach actually moves much but it's a start.

"At the same time," he emphasizes, "Squeeze your

butt just a little so your hips tilt forward."

I move my hips forward and back, trying to figure out what the hell he's talking about.

"You ready? Let's try it. We're in what's called a plank position. You're going to feel it all over your body but I want you to concentrate on feeling it in your shoulders. Got it?"

"Oh yeah," I pant out. "I feel it."

"Now slowly lower yourself to the ground and push back up. Stay in this plank position. The only movement should be the bend in your arms."

I make it to the bottom and grunt as I push myself back up. I let my stomach go long ago and no idea if my butt ever squeezed at all, but I make it. I have to pant a few times before trying again. Down is easier this time, but coming back up is significantly harder.

"Aaaaaahhhhhhhh!" I yell as I push, elated when I make it to the top even if I'm not sure what my form looks like.

"What are you doing?"

I scramble to my feet as soon as I hear her voice, embarrassed to have been caught.

"Working out." I grab my glasses off the coffee table and put them on quickly.

When I can finally see Nicole, I notice the confusion written all over her face. "But… why?"

I sniff and push my scraggly hair off my forehead. "You know, to get muscles and to like, get fit. Cause I'm a man."

She comes closer and I can't help noticing her beautiful blue eyes. They're one of the things I love most about her. I can always tell her mood by how bright they are. Right now, they look happy. That's exactly how I wanted them to look when I made her move in with Kiersten and Paul. I'm glad it worked.

"Kade, you don't need to get fit. You're perfect the way you are."

"Don't push it today, gentlemen," the guy on the TV yells. "Just do five. We'll build up as we go. Remember, this is called *Pushups for Beginners* for a reason."

Mortified that she now knows I'm basically subscribing to a Workout for Dummies channel, I snatch the remote off the couch and shut everything off. I feel the heat rising on my face as my cheeks turn red.

"Are you doing this for me?" she asks quietly.

Hands on my hips, I keep my gaze focused on the floor. I want her to know I'm trying to be the man she needs. That I want more than anything to be good enough for her. But I'm not sure I'll ever be able to do enough push-ups to even be able to buck up to a random person and intimidate them if they want to hit on her. So, I don't answer her question, instead deflecting.

"How did you get here? Don't you have security detail following you?"

"Kiersten brought me." Nicole winds around the couch and sits down patting the cushion next to hers. I leave that one in between us and opt for the furthest away seat instead. If I get close enough to smell her shampoo, I'll cave and it's too important to keep her safe. Besides, I don't smell like any form of shampoo at all after working out. Just one more thing to be embarrassed about around her.

"Doesn't sound very safe to be driving around like that."

"You're right. Riding in a car is one of the unsafest things any of us could do these days. Car accidents are everywhere."

I know she's trying to make me smile, but it makes my frown deeper instead.

"That's not what I meant."

"I know. But I'm trying to put it into perspective."

"By trying to convince me that the possibility of a car wreck is at all the same as a guy we know is trying to target you and harm you purposely?"

"No." She leans in, adding strength to her words. "By reminding you that there are no guarantees on any of our safety. Ever. That's the point I keep trying to make with everyone." She throws her hands up in exasperation. "I don't want to live with this fear hanging over my head anymore. I want to live my life to the fullest. Does that mean there will be some risks involved? Of course. But it's worth it to me and I'm tired of everyone else deciding how my life is going to go."

"I thought we sorted all that out a couple of days ago at the meeting."

"*They* did," she emphasizes. "*You* didn't."

Surprised, I finally look up at her and see calm all over her face. "What do you mean?"

"I notice your roommate hasn't moved in."

I turn my eyes away, ashamed to have been caught in my lie.

Nicole scoots forward until our knees are touching, the contact making my body tingle. But I resist touching her back. I'm no good for her.

"Kade, I know you're trying to protect me by sacrificing your own happiness. But that's not how this works."

Deflect, deflect, deflect...

"I don't know what you mean."

"I think you do," she argues. For the first time, I'm starting to think she may not let this go without a real fight.

"I think you love me so much you'll do anything for me. Even if it means making up a story about your old roommate coming back so I'm forced to move somewhere that you think I'll be safe."

I stand up quickly, unsure how to feel about the fact that she pegged my motivations so easily.

"The crazy thing is," she continues as she stands up as well, "The safest place I've ever felt is here, with you."

"That's ridiculous."

"It's not." She moves close enough to put her hands on my chest. "Kade, I love you."

In my shock, my eyes whip up to look into hers.

She loves me?

"You love me?"

"So much."

I slowly point a finger at my chest, thoroughly confused. "Me?"

A smile graces her beautiful face. "You."

"But why?"

"Because you're kind and caring. You're hard-working and funny. I love playing video games with you even if I'm terrible at them. And I've never felt so safe with anyone in my life. I know you'd rather cut off your arm than ever hurt me. You always put me first and you can read me like a book."

I take a step back, overwhelmed by this… this… list she's made of my attributes. None of this is any big deal. It's just human decency. She can't love me because of basic things that everyone should do.

"Kade, I know this is scary, but the world is scary. All of it. The only time I'm not scared at all, that I'm totally reassured everything is going to be okay, is when I'm with you."

I shake my head, still in disbelief of everything she's saying. "You should be with some rich guy who can drape you in the finest clothes and cover you in jewelry. Who can give you a house behind a gate."

"No Kade," she forces herself back into my space and I'm powerless to stop her now. Being away from her has been torture. I don't think I can resist her for much longer. "I should be with the man who loves me as much as I love him." She bites her bottom lip and I'm a goner. Yet I can't find it in me to care. "That's you, isn't it?"

Staring at her lips that keep inching closer, I nod. "Yes, that's me. I love you, Nicole."

I can't stop the words. Can't stop the movement. I should resist, but I can't. I don't want to. It hurts too much to be without her.

"I know."

Our lips finally fuse together and it's as if everything she's said, every argument she's made as to why we are supposed to be together finally sinks into me on the cellular level. As we kiss, everything suddenly makes sense. And I know with everything in me that she's right.

We're meant to be together, so together we will be.

I'm so deep into the feeling of her lips on mine, her tongue caressing mine, her body next to mine, it comes as a shock when her cold hands touch the skin on my back.

"Holy shit," I accidentally exclaim making her giggle.

"Sorry. Should I warm them up first?"

I unwrap her arms from around my waist and cup her small hands in mine, blowing warm air onto them and rubbing her fingers until they're warm. She bites her bottom lip, never taking her eyes off mine and something stirs deep inside me. It's a longing like I've never felt before. I don't want to push her, but if she'll have me, every single part of me that no one has ever had before, I'll never be able to let her go again.

"There. That's better."

I release her hands and she immediately slides them under my shirt again, feeling every inch of skin, all the way up to my shoulders. When she reaches the top, she pushes at my shirt and before I can think too much about it, I help her take it off.

Standing before her, I feel my cheeks begin to flame. I've never taken my shirt off in front of anyone before. Not even to go swimming. I'm hardly naked, but I feel exposed. She's seeing the parts of me that I keep hidden for a reason.

"What?" She is always able to gauge my mood more than anyone. "Why won't you look at me?"

"I just…" I stammer as I try to keep myself under control. I want to throw my shirt on and run away but I'm trying to concentrate on the fact that we might have sex and I don't want to miss it. "Um… my muscles are just really shy and like to hide under all the fluff."

Nicole's face breaks out into a brilliant smile, but then her eyes darken a bit. There's a hunger in them. She licks her lips and I know instinctually that I need to prepare myself for what's about to happen.

Slowly, achingly so, she kisses my chin… my neck… the spot right under my ear that has me letting out a groan I didn't know I had in me. But she's not done. She continues her kisses and small nibbles down my chest where she lightly bites my nipple.

"Oh, God!" I call out and I can feel her chuckle as she keeps going, down my lack-of-abs and right to the happy trail I'm sporting.

She finally stops to look up at me and holy hell, just

knowing how close her mouth is to my dick makes me closer to coming in my pants than I feel comfortable with.

"Uh… what are you… I mean… what…"

Her fingers slide into the waistband of my pants, so deep I can feel the heat of her fingers on my tip. My eyes roll back before I can stop them, but Nicole doesn't go any further. Instead, she has pity on me and stands up to kiss me again.

Hand still in my pants, she leans back. "Have you ever done this before?"

My breath comes in pants as I shake my head, too amped up on sexual adrenaline to care that I just admitted to being a virgin.

"Do you want to do this?"

I nod rapidly, my eyes glued to hers, wondering what she'll do next. What move she'll make that will be my un-doing.

"Do you have a condom?"

I pause to think. Is the box still in my nightstand, stored there based on a hope and a prayer that someday I'd need them? And are they expired at this point? "I think so."

She runs her other hand up my arm and around my neck, playing with the short strands of my hair. It's a good thing she asked the condom question already because my brain has officially shut off.

"It's okay. We can have some fun without them this time, if we need to."

My mouth drops open at the suggestiveness of her words. This is a side of Nicole I never expected to see. My beautiful, gentle, would never utter a curse-word girl is a sex kitten when she gets turned on. And she's turned on by *me*!

All I can do is nod again, dying to know what she

means by fun without birth control. The visual images I conjure up do nothing to calm my hormones. Oh shit, this is going to be quick. I already know it.

Walking backward, Nicole leads me by my waistband to my bedroom. Not that she needs to keep ahold of me. I'd follow her no matter what, but I'm glad she did. There is something wildly sexy by her guiding me around with her hand on my fly.

I'll have to explore that thought later, maybe when I'm not about to have sex for the first time.

"Where do you think those condoms are?"

I point to my nightstand, completely incapable of forming sentences at this point.

She finds them quickly, immediately scanning the package like she read my mind about the expiration date issue. By the quirk of her eyebrow, I can only assume they're still good.

"Well," she tosses the package on the bed. "Looks like we can have as much or as little fun as you want. What do you want, Kade?"

I swallow hard and croak out, "You."

"Good." Her facial expression immediately changes and the girl I've come to love is back. "Listen, if you don't want to go all the way, we don't have to. This isn't about sex. I love you, Kade. That's what it's about. Nothing more, nothing less."

If I wasn't already putty in her hands, I certainly am now. "I love you, too. And I want to. I really do. But what if I'm no good at it?"

"Then we have reason to practice more, right?" She shrugs slyly. "Sex isn't about good or bad." She thinks for a second. "I mean it is… sort of. But not in the way you think. Not for me anyway. It's about love and connection and two people who are the best of friends taking their feelings for each other even further. That's what it's about for me."

"I understand. I do. I just… want to be better than anyone you've ever been with."

There. I said it. I admit to having a slight bit of jealousy that she's done this before with other people. I have no idea where that caveman thought process even came from but it's true.

Nicole, understanding as always, reaches up on her toes to kiss me softly.

"I've only been with one other person, Kade. And you know how that ended."

My nostrils flare as Jeremy's name flashes through my mind. Fuck him for taking such a precious thing from her and taking it for granted in the worst way.

She cups my cheek. "But he's not here. Kade." She waits for me to make eye contact. "Don't bring him in this room with us."

I take a couple of seconds to center myself because she's right. Nothing and no one should be in this room with us. This is about her and I.

I lean down and take her lips again, no longer nervous to lick the seam and tangle her tongue with mine. I stay focused on the feel of her as any thoughts I had fade away again, focused only on the woman that I love.

Sensing my continued hesitation at doing something wrong, she takes a few steps back and pulls her shirt over her head. I practically choke on my tongue at the sight of her pale pink bra, so thin I can see the color of her nipples through it.

"Holy shit," I breathe.

But she's not done. She wiggles out of her pants revealing matching panties. My eyes travel back and forth between the nipples I can see and the neat line of hair revealed between her legs.

I feel myself sway for just a second, overcome by the gravity of this moment and how she's baring herself, her whole self, to me. No hesitation, no concerns, sheer love in her eyes.

Slowly, she reaches behind her to unclasp her bra. When it falls to the floor in front of her, I almost pass out from the vision. When the panties are gone, any thoughts disappear with them. I'm a goner. I am one hundred percent in her control now. There's no going back. Everything I know, everything I feel for her has changed. The intensity of my emotions is nothing I've ever felt before. And we haven't even had sex yet.

Her hips swaying as she moves, Nicole returns to me and makes quick work of removing my pants. For one split second, I realize I'm naked in front of someone for the very first time and I consider sucking in my gut. But then she grabs my dick gently and it feels like a lightning bolt just flashed through my entire body.

Somehow my forehead ends up resting on her shoulder as she strokes me up and down. "That feels so much different than when I do it."

"Better, I hope." There's a hint of amusement in her voice.

"So much better. Maybe a little too good." I don't want her to ever stop, but I also know there're even better things to come if I don't, well, come. "I don't want it to end like this."

I groan as she removes her hand and grabs both of mine. "Then let's move this to the bed, shall we?"

I stumble for a second, forgetting my pants are still

down around my ankles. Quickly, I get them all the way off, dying to know what she has in mind for our next step. I don't have to wait to find out.

"I know you're nervous about this being good for me." I nod because yes. It would absolutely suck to know I'm a terrible lover, especially the first time I try it. "Would you like me to take the lead this time?"

"Yes, please."

Her answering kiss is all I need to know it doesn't matter if I'm a passive participant this time. She's going to make sure it's wonderful for both of us.

"Lay down on your back," she demands, my eyes widening for a brief second before I do as she says.

Climbing over top of me, she kisses her way up my chest as my eyes stay trained on her breasts, swaying with her movement. Taking a chance that I can't do this wrong, I reach up and brush my fingers over her hard nipples. When she gasps, I can only assume it's in pleasure, so I do it again.

She situates herself on my lap, my dick so close to her core, I can feel her heat, and closes her eyes while I play with her beautiful tits. I rub her nipples between my thumb and forefinger, watching the reactions on her face as I find what she likes.

So engrossed in my exploration, I jolt when her hand finds my dick again and she rolls a condom on. Somehow in my enjoyment of just touching her, I didn't even notice her reach for the box.

My hands drop to the bed as I wait with anticipation to see what she's going to do next. I'm not disappointed. Sitting up on her knees, she raises me up and lines my tip with her entrance. Moving it back and forth, she coats me with her wetness before sinking down on me.

I groan loudly as she lowers herself all the way until we're hip to hip. And then she stills.

When I'm finally able to open my eyes again, I look up at her. She's quite pleased with my reaction to this moment which makes me puff out a chuckle. The movement causes me to move inside her and I gasp at how such a small move can bring me such a massive amount of pleasure.

"Congratulations on being deflowered," she jokes and I dare not laugh again for fear this will be over before it has even really begun. "I'm going to take this really slow to try and make it last, okay?" I barely nod, trusting her to do all the moving.

She sees it though, and ever so slowly, lifts up drawing me right out of her, before slowly sitting again. She continues with her movement, a look of ecstasy on her face and I have to close my eyes from the visual images that are assaulting me and just *feel*.

My whole body is strung tight and I'm not sure how long I can last. Especially when she moves her hips side to side, riding me with such precision I can't stop myself from grabbing her hips and pulling her tight to me.

My hips begin moving, tiny thrusts I can't control as she rocks and sways, her fingertips digging into my chest to steady herself.

"Nicole… I… Oh, god…" I pant, feeling a change coming that I'm unable to stop or slow down.

"I know. Don't hold back," she breathes heavily. "I'm close, too. Give me your hand."

I obey and she licks my thumb before placing it at the juncture of her thighs, never slowing her movement.

"Rub," she demands and like the obedient man I am, I do. "Gently. Oh, god that's good. Keep doing that."

My thumb moves faster and faster, my hips still thrusting, and in what seems like no time at all and yet forever of anticipation, she cries out, her insides squeezing me as she comes.

Two thrusts later, an explosion like I've never felt runs through my entire body, my brain bursting with sparks only I can see.

As I linger in the intensity of my first sexual experience, unable to form complete thoughts, I know deep down to my core that I will never be the same. I am done for. She is mine. And I will never let go of her again.

TWENTY-NINE
Nicole

Tangled up in the sheets with Kade is exactly where I was hoping to be. I can tell he's still a little nervous, but he's definitely more relaxed since having an orgasm. I'll have to remember that for the future.

I giggle to myself at the thought.

"What?" Kade's fingers lightly graze my shoulder as we rest.

"Nothing. Just thinking about how I'll have to do that again next time you're tense."

He guffaws. "Uh, I have no problem with you doing that again for any reason."

I turn my head on his shoulder so I can look up at him. "Was your first time everything you imagined it would be?"

"Nope," he says with no hesitation.

"What? Seriously?"

"Yep. It was so much better." Kade pinches my chin between his thumb and forefinger and leans down to kiss me again. A girl could get used to this.

Laying back down I sigh heavily. "I don't want to get out of this bed."

"Wanna do it again instead?"

I snort with laughter. "You're already recovered enough?"

I'm not totally sure since I'm at an awkward angle, but I'd bet money the look on his face says I've lost my mind.

"I have been waiting my entire life to be naked in bed with the hottest woman I've ever known. I am absolutely recovered enough. Watching you come was more amazing than any porn I've ever watched. You've ruined those movies for me."

I try hard not to cover my face with embarrassment. I am fully aware that I'm a lady on the streets and a vixen in the sheets.

"Wait. Don't you have class?"

I grimace even though he can't see me from this angle and definitely not without his glasses. "I sort of skipped today."

"Nicole!"

"It was too important to make things right with you. Besides, I have a ninety-seven in the class so far. I'll catch up."

"Fine. I'll let it slide this time. But please don't let me be your excuse for not following your dreams. Promise me."

His words warm my insides. Knowing he wants me to be the best version of myself that I can be, isn't that what every woman wants from the man they love?

"I promise."

"Good. But tonight, that means staying in this bed, naked, since there's nowhere else we need to be."

"Well, at some point, when we both have a night off,

we need to take down that dead Christmas tree out there. I know the holidays are far from over, but that sucker didn't make it."

"Don't remind me," he groans. "Next year, we're going with a fake tree. All the way." He suddenly stills. "I mean, you know. If you're still dating me or whatever."

I ignore the insecurity in his voice, knowing most of it stems from a habit I want to help him break. "You better make sure I go with you to pick it out. After this year, I think you might need a little extra advice and I happen to be a Christmas expert."

"Oh, you are, are you?" He pinches my side making me giggle.

"I am. But before we talk about next year, and before we do it again," that gets a happy moan from him. "We probably need to go get my stuff out of the car."

I know I just ripped the band-aid off on a new topic of conversation, but I can't avoid it forever. He rolls to face me, forcing me to move from my comfortable spot. "Wait, I thought you said Kiersten drove you. Did someone pick her up?"

I scowl. I knew he'd catch that. "I may have told a little white lie."

He flops back on the bed. "Nicole. Do I need to kick you out again?"

"No. Listen." I nudge him. "She knew I was coming. It's not a big deal."

He pops back up, poised to argue. "It *is* a big deal. Jeremy is still out there."

"Actually, he's not."

That stops him. This is new information he doesn't know yet. I barely even know. "What?"

Sitting up, I tuck the sheet under my arms, having discovered Kade's obsession with my boobs and knowing we'll never get through this conversation if I'm not at least somewhat covered up. As much as I'd like a replay, this is too important for all our peace of mind.

"I got a call from the assistant DA before I came over. Jeremy accepted the plea deal."

"Wait… wait, wait." He pushes himself up to lean on the headboard and grabs his glasses. "I thought you had to go to the trial to testify or something."

"The plea bargain means there won't be a trial at all so I didn't have to go."

"What was the deal?"

This is the hard part. It's not great, but there's nothing I can do about it.

"Brace yourself," I warn. "He gets three months of jail time, a couple hundred hours of community service, and two years probation."

"Three months? That's it?"

I can already hear Kade's anger ramping up, not that I blame him. Jeremy's issue didn't just affect me. He changed the lives of all the people around me as well.

"I know it's not a lot. But I told you guys this before. He's a white frat boy with country club parents and no prior record. I'm surprised he got any jail time at all, to be honest."

"That's just…" Kade shakes his head dejectedly. "It's not fair."

"It never is. But the point is, he's already in custody and his time starts today. For the next three months at least, we can all get back to normal for a while."

"And then what? We look over our shoulders again? I don't like it."

I rest my hand on his upper thigh and don't miss the

flare of lust in his eyes. It's only there for a second, but I see it. I also make a mental note to remember what my touch does to him, at least while he's still new to this whole sex thing.

"Neither do I. But it's what we have to deal with and I'm not going to let him stop our lives because he's decided to stay in town for whatever reason. We don't even know if he'll be back when he gets out. Faith could have broken up with him or whatever and he won't have any reason to come here."

"Except to stalk you."

I cock my head with understanding because he's right about that part. "Maybe. But I'll just keep documenting that he's teetering the line of violating the order so when it comes up for renewal, I'll have solid evidence that he's still a credible threat."

Kade shakes his head and runs his hand down his face, obviously unhappy with this turn of events.

"Hey. Look at me."

He complies, fear in his eyes. "I just got you. I'm afraid I'm going to lose you."

"Because of Jeremy or just because?"

He has to think on that one for a second. But to his credit, he answers honestly. "Just because, I guess."

I scoot forward a bit, still holding onto the sheet. "I told you before, and I'll keep saying it until you believe me. I love you, Kade. I love the way you treat people and the way you laugh and the way you bring peace and calm and stability to my life."

"Even if I never make a lot of money and we live in an apartment forever?"

"Even if we live in a box, I will still love you."

His lips quirk up on the side. "Let's just stick to the

apartment for now."

"Agreed."

"And Nicole?"

"Yeah?"

His hand cups my cheek and I let the sheet go, knowing instinctively where this is headed. "Thank you for loving me. I really love you, too. Always have. Always will."

He kisses me gently a few times before his movements turn reverent again. I spend the next several hours showing him how much I love him with my touch, no more words needed.

THIRTY
Nicole

6 months later

Trotting down the sidewalk, I don't dare slow my steps. Today is an exciting day. Thank goodness my classes end at two so I can get home. There's a lot to do and not much time to do it.

Getting to the parking lot, I stop dead in my tracks when I see Jeremy leaning against his black truck. My heart rate begins to pick up but I quickly redirect my thoughts, like Dr. Rhonda and I have been working on.

Breathe in, two, three, four…

He won't hurt me.

…hold, two, three, four…

He can't control me anymore.

… and out, two, three, four…

He is an insignificant part of your day.

…hold, two, three, four…

Quickly, my heart rate returns to normal so I pull out my camera and take a picture of how close he is and make sure there is a time and date stamp before moving it to the folder on my phone that connects automatically to a dropbox.

He's been back for a few months now and I guess he and Faith are still together. As I watch her walk toward him, a wave of sadness hits me. It's June and summer is making sure we know she's on her way with more heat and humidity.

And Faith is wearing long sleeves and a scarf. I know why and I wish I could make her see reason, but I can't make someone leave if they aren't ready. I can only hope she saved my number from when we were lab partners and will use it when she is finally ready to protect herself.

I gesture my head in greeting at her, knowing she won't respond. She never does and I don't expect her to. I'm sure it's dangerous for her to acknowledge me.

They climb into his truck and I watch as he peels out of the parking lot, the sounds of his car likely the only way he can express his anger at my refusal to let him control me. Dr. Rhonda and I have talked a lot about it and if he can't use his words or fists to express his anger toward me, he'll find another way to let me know. I can only assume the squealing tires and revving engine are it.

Kade thinks I should be more on alert, but right now, I don't feel like I'm in danger. The worse that happens is the automatic adrenaline kick I get when I see him unexpectedly, but even that is getting easier to control. If Jeremy gets any closer than the back of the parking lot while he waits for Faith, it'll be a different story. And yes, I know he's technically violating the order, but the whole purpose was to keep him away from me. Since he does, I'm letting it ride.

Climbing in my car, I toss my bag onto the seat next to me and crank the engine, grateful the A/C blows cool air almost immediately. June is nice, but it still gets hot inside a closed car in Central Texas.

I make my way back to the apartment Kade and I still share, although we sleep in the same bedroom now. Unsurprisingly, the extra bedroom turned into the XBOX room complete with a couple of gaming chairs I sprang for as a late Christmas present and the whole console set up he sprang for shortly after. Kade loves it. Unless Carson is spending the night and he has to sleep in the bed we still have stored in that room. Then Kade rethinks the whole idea of our new setup.

I've gotten really good at distracting him when he can't play his beloved video games, though. He complains a lot less now that he knows putting the handset down means he can do other things with his fingers.

All his fears about not being good in bed? Totally unwarranted. Kade is the most generous lover a girl could ask for.

Tossing my keys on the counter when I walk into the apartment and dropping my bag by the couch, I know exactly where my boyfriend is by the yelling coming from the other room.

"Archie, you asshole, how did you miss jumping back on your horse? It's a two-foot jump."

I peek my head in the door, and sure enough, he's leaning forward in his chair, obviously engaged in some sort of train heist.

"Hey."

"Hey." He doesn't even look up as his thumbs move in rapid time. His biceps flex from the movement and I swell with pride at how far he's come.

After I walked in on Kade learning how to do pushups, he sheepishly admitted it's something he's always wanted to master. So, I encouraged him to continue and promised not to be in the room while he practiced until he was ready.

He's up to thirty pushups in a row now without so much as breaking a sweat or making me move off the couch when he does it. It doesn't matter to me that he can do them now, but it makes him feel good about himself and that's what really matters.

Also, I don't hate the way short sleeves look on him. Not at all.

"We have to leave in thirty," I remind him, curious if he's even listening.

"Kay. Go, Matty! Go! Got the bag of money?"

"And we're supposed to bring that ring box in the top dresser drawer."

"Kay. Got it! Good job guys."

"And a spaceship landed in the middle of campus and beamed up a bunch of people."

"Cool. Do you see a sheriff? I have a gut feeling guys. We need to keep our eyes open."

Rolling my own eyes at the fact that he's obviously not listening to me, I sit in the spare gaming chair, put on the headset and flip on the remote.

"Hey, Nicole's here! Hey Nic!"

I smile at the sound of his voice. "Hey Matty. Shouldn't you be in school?"

"Exempt from all my finals."

"So, you've just been sitting around playing *Red Dead Redemption* all day?"

"What else is there to do?" he asks like the high school senior who is ready for graduation next week that he is.

"Plenty. In fact, I'm going to have to grab my boyfriend because we have plans." I turn my character to shoot Kade's avatar in the back with a shotgun, killing him on the spot.

"Who shot me?" Kade yells. "Where is he?"

"Right behind you babe."

The look on his face is so comical, I can't help but laugh. "What? You killed me? What was that for?"

"When I told you all about the aliens on campus and you didn't flinch, I just knew you forgot that we have plans in twenty-five minutes."

Kade grabs his phone and looks at the time. "Shit. You're right. I gotta go guys."

He's answered with a chorus of kissy noises and "he's so whipped" as he leaves the game. Kade used to be embarrassed by it but quickly decided his friends are just jealous and didn't that just boost his ego a bit.

"Hey babe," he finally says once the handset is set aside, actually putting his attention on me. Leaning over, he gives me a kiss, lingering just a bit while I scratch at the scruff on his face. "How was class?"

"Fine. Math. I hate it."

"If you need help, you can always ask."

As it turns out, Kade is better at math than he gave himself credit for until his adviser suggested he consider a career in something math-based like accounting. He's still technically undecided but is leaning in that direction when he has to declare a major. He doesn't mind all the numbers and has gotten a bit cocky about how easy it comes to him if you ask me. I love it of course. It's nice seeing him have the confidence he never had before.

"I'll be fine. No need to throw your calculator brain in my face."

He snorts a laugh and pulls me to my feet so we can get ready.

"Fine, fine. You're on your own. What time do we have

to be there?"

"It's about a twenty-minute drive and we need to be there by three."

"So, I have time to shower?"

"You do. I don't. Jump in while I touch up my makeup and stuff."

He smacks me on the ass, his second favorite part of my body after my boobs. "It'll just take me a second."

It takes him longer than a second but we're at least both ready and out the door on time. It takes a little longer to get into the courthouse than I expected once we find a parking space and get through security, but we still make it.

"NicNic!" Carson yells and runs over wrapping his arms around my legs before pulling back and looking up at me. "You look pwetty, Nic."

"Why thank you." I do a little shimmy in my short satiny blue frock. "And don't you look handsome in your suit and tie."

"I don't like the tie, Nic." He yanks on it gently so I pretend to loosen it, mostly to keep his hands from messing it up.

"Does that feel better?"

"Yeah."

And then he's back to his parents, tie forgotten about.

"How are you feeling?" I ask my sister as I give her a hug and hand her the bouquet that's been in my fridge since this morning. "Nervous?"

"About being married? No. About getting in there before they close for the night? Yes."

I fiddle with her hair, making sure it's all in place. "You already have your reservation. They aren't going to leave before doing your ceremony."

"Rationally, I know that," she says as she bats my hand

away. "But nothing ever seems to go the way I want it to, so I'm mentally preparing myself for the worst."

"She's been at it all day," Paul interjects, putting his arm around her waist. He's looking just as dapper as Carson in a suit almost identical to my nephew's. "I keep telling her everything is going to be fine but you know how she is sometimes."

"Worried that the bottom will drop out on the best day of my life? Yeah. I know," she freely admits. "But we're still missing half our people so can you blame me?"

"Yes," Lauren says as she comes up from behind. "I told you we'd be here. And we are."

There are hugs and hand slaps all around as Lauren, Heath, Annika, and Jaxon join our little group in the hallway.

"Willoughby-Franklin wedding!"

The yell from the doorway of the courtroom has us all jumping into motion. In a matter of seconds, Paul is standing at the front of the room, the guys all next to him. Annika and Lauren are standing on the other side and as Annika starts the music on her phone, I walk down the short aisle and take my place.

Carson marches in next and walks straight to Lauren like he was told to do. It wasn't a fight to get him there. Lauren is still his favorite babysitter. Next to me, of course.

Then it's my sister's turn. She looks amazing. Her long dark hair is pinned back in loose waves down her back. A short, simple A-line dress showing off her figure and mostly her legs.

But I'm not watching her. I'm watching Paul. It doesn't matter that he already saw her in the dress. It doesn't matter that they've been living together for over a year. He can barely hold back the tears as he watches her walk toward him, ready to join him in marriage.

The judge goes through the rigmarole of marrying them, but I'm hardly listening, too busy taking in the joy on the faces of everyone I love.

And then… the words are finally said.

"I now pronounce you husband and wife. You may kiss your bride."

We cheer as Paul takes Kiersten in his arms and dips her in a dramatic fashion. The longer they stay that way, the more impatient Carson gets. Finally, he's had enough.

Tugging on Paul's sleeve, he interrupts. "Mom. Dad. You're done. Let's go."

I can't help the giggle that escapes me at his demands. I'm not the only one. Heath grabs Carson and tosses him in the air, making him squeal with delight.

I catch Kade's eye as he stands chatting with Jaxon. I feel like such a lucky woman to have found a man like him. He's not the most athletic. He doesn't own a business. He's not going to be a doctor. But he's the perfect man for me. And someday, surrounded by our friends and family, we'll end up as happy and content as my sister just did. I know it with everything in me.

It's just a matter of time.

The End.

EPILOGUE
Ellery

Grabbing my purse, I swing the door of my smart Kia Sorrento open and run for the door. It's pointless. Even parked in the front row, the rain is so heavy I'm drenched by the time I'm standing under the awning.

"Great," I mutter and try to smooth my hair. Not that it matters. The tight chignon I wear to be professional at work isn't going anywhere. No, it just lost any volume I had on the top. Figures.

Sighing, I pull open the heavy door and step inside.

"Whoa." This not at all what I expected to find. The large open space has dim lighting, but it's still bright enough to see. The walls are a pale gray with black accents everywhere, including the front of the large bar. Modern furnishings are scattered around the room, inviting people to sit and stay awhile.

All the large vehicles in the parking lot suddenly make sense when I notice the customers. There are lots of couples here, but most of them are grouped together in cliques, and all of the men are huge. Not that everyone isn't huge compared to me. At just over five feet, I tend to dwarf just about everyone. But these men are different. Even sitting down, I can tell almost all of them are well over six feet.

I'm surprised to see the bartender is a woman about my age, although I'm not sure why I'm surprised. Maybe I've been in the corporate world long enough, I forgot other people still work to live instead of vice versa.

Making my way to the counter, I slide onto the stool, noticing how much more comfortable the seat is than I anticipated.

Wow. This is such a fancy place. I wonder why the outside is so dingy and non-descript. Seems like they could get a lot more business if they gave the outside a fresh coat of paint and made the sign easier to read.

I don't notice the bartender, too busy taking in the environment, until she's standing right in front of me.

"Welcome to Frui Vita. What can I get you?" I'm struck by how beautiful she is with her long dark hair and lean body. Even the act of tossing a napkin down in front of me seems somehow graceful when she does it. I'm suddenly feeling very intimidated and unsure of myself.

"Um… I think I'd like… uh…" I stumble over my words as I try to remember what, if any kind of alcohol I've tried and liked before. I appreciate she just stands there patiently while I try to decide. "Whiskey, straight up," I finally say.

This elicits an eyebrow raise from her making me second guess myself.

"That's not the right answer, is it?" I ask quietly.

She smiles kindly at my complete ineptness when it comes to alcohol consumption. "There's not really a right or wrong answer but… well… can I ask you a question?"

I nod vigorously.

"You don't drink very often do you?"

My nod turns into a shake.

"And I'm guessing from looking at you, today's been a really hard day and you're just trying to take the edge off."

I release a deep breath, my shoulders slumping. "Is it that obvious?"

"Only because we've all been there. Driving around in the rain so you don't have to go home. Finally ending up in some random bar ready to drink your night away."

I feel my eyes widen. "Really? I'm not the only one?"

She bobbles her head back and forth. "Plus, you've got the splotchy eyes. I hate getting those things."

My hands cover my face, not that they can wipe away the red splotches I didn't realize were there. "Oh my gosh, I didn't know I looked that bad."

"You don't. I promise. I'm just a woman, too. We can see these things in each other." She leans on the counter, fingers clasped together. "And let me just say, woman to woman, whoever he is, he didn't deserve you."

I feel my eyes well with tears again, not out of sadness, but grateful for her kindness. "Thank you. I haven't quite decided how I feel yet."

"You will. In the meantime," she pushes off the bar and reaches for a glass. "I'm going to make you an amaretto sour, light on the amaretto. I know you want to drink your cares away, but I think taking the edge off is probably more your style."

Oddly, I feel some relief that she's not encouraging me to do anything rash like taking shots or do a keg stand or something. Physically, I could do it, that wouldn't be a problem. But I still have to work tomorrow morning. I don't need to smell like stale booze when I walk by Mrs.

Welch in the hallway. As it is, I'm not even positive I still have a job now that Kevin and I aren't together. This is the curse of working for your boyfriend – er, ex-boyfriend's mother.

The bartender, whose name I should probably ask at some point, places a small glass of yellowish-orange liquid in front of me. I like that it has a small orange slice attached to the rim. It's a funny thing to appreciate, but right now, it seems like the little things are more important than ever.

Taking a sip through the tiny straw, my mouth is flooded with flavor. "Mmm," I remark and take another sip.

"Hits the spot, right?" she asks with a smile, although I'm not sure if she's pleased with herself for having guessed correctly or if she's genuinely happy she put a smile on my face.

"It really does. Thank you."

"No problem. If you need anything else, just holler."

She leaves me to my thoughts that I try to keep solidly out of the breakup zone and fully engaged in observing the people around me. Not only are all the men huge, everyone looks like they have money. I don't mean the decent amount I get paid as an accountant, but lots of money. Like in the millions.

My gaze zeros in on one man in particular. He's at least six-four. The grey tailored suit he's wearing shows off his broad shoulders and tapered waist. His hair is cropped close to his head and dark scruff covers his face. A face that has scars and a large bruise on one cheek.

He is both terrifying and sexy as all get out.

And he's walking right toward me.

ACKNOWLEDGMENTS

The last couple of years have been rough on everyone. For those of us already working from home in a job they love, you would think the shift of life would be no big deal. Unfortunately, we weren't immune from the massive life changes as well.

For those of you who kept my spirits up and motivated me to keep going, I thank you. This book wouldn't have been written without you.

For those of you who had a hand in this book's development and publishing, I am forever grateful.

9 781948 852326